Wollaston
Libra.,

This book is due for return on or before the last date shown below.

IN THE SAME SERIES

MindF**k

FANIE VILJOEN

MindF**k

FANIE VILJOEN

Series Editor: Peter Lancett

Published by Ransom Publishing Ltd.
Radley House, 8 St. Cross Road, Winchester, Hampshire, SO23 9HX, UK
www.ransom.co.uk

ISBN 978 184167 9945

First published in 2010
Copyright © 2010 Fanie Viljoen.
Front cover photograph: Frederick Nacino

For the broken and the beaten –
when the music is all you've got left,
crank the volume right up.

Warning

This book won't make you feel better about yourself, it won't explain the meaning of life, and it certainly won't help you 'find' yourself. If Mommy and Daddy don't like it when you read books with explicit language do one of the following right now:

- Chuck the damn book away.

- Kindly request the bookshop where you bought the book to exchange it for one of those transform-your-life-into-something-precious-and-beautiful-in-ten-easy-steps-books.

- If you nicked the book from a bookshop, return it in the same fashion and instead nick one of those transform-your-life-into-something-precious-and-beautiful-in-ten-easy-steps-books.

- You can tear out the pages and use them to smoke a little something.

- You can secretly read the book in the loo where Mommy and Daddy will (hopefully) not disturb you.

If you still have the book in your hands, you probably want to continue reading it. Then, my bru, you're in for a hell of a ride, but be warned: this book is going to mess with your mind and it may just leave you even more fucked-up than you already are.

press **play** to begin . . .

TRACK 01

The things we won't do for money

It was Friday night. I sent an SMS to Kerbs:

> 2night, 12 bells. bring ur tools. i'l open the hate.

'Open the hate, what hate?' grunted Kerbs while slipping through the gate. The rain poured down and shined on his jacket.

'Hate?'

'The SMS, dude'

'The gate, Kerbs!'

'You really should learn how to fucking spell, Burns.'

'Yeah, the day you find a job.'

It had been a year now since Kerbs finished school, and he was still unemployed. I always reckoned that anyone who even considered giving him a job would be totally off their rocker.

'Yeah, right,' said Kerbs.

Back to business: Everything was organised. I nicked three of my mom's sleeping pills earlier that night. One for the mutt. (He'd chowed down hard on that vienna and by now he was in doggy dreamland.) One for the old man. (He knocked back the whiskey and should be hanging around alcoholic heaven roundabout now.) Last but not least, one for my mom – in her coffee. I think she had already popped one by herself as well, but I wasn't going to take any chances. (She was probably so wired that we would only see her later the following afternoon.) Kelly missed the drug party. (She was with her boyfriend again.)

'Come on, I'm getting soaked,' I said to Kerbs.

He walked up to my mom's brand new BMW in the driveway. 'Is the alarm off?'

I pressed the button on the remote. The car's lights flashed and the doors jumped open, but we couldn't take the easy road. It would look too suspicious.

It was the perfect night to put our plan into action: Mom forgot to park the car in the garage. She'd intended going to the gym but it had probably slipped her mind. The rain also helped; the neighbours would be sound asleep. And nobody would show their faces to investigate strange noises.

Kerbs stood ready with a brick in his hand. His gaze met mine. I nodded. With great force he hurled the brick through the car's passenger window. The glass shattered, shooting away like stars and falling on the wet paving. Only then did he open the door.

'Do you know what you're doing?' I asked.

'Sort of.'

He got into the car and wedged a screwdriver between the Kenwood front loader CD player and the dashboard. It wasn't easy, but he didn't take any shit. I could hear the dashboard cracking. With the tip of the screwdriver lodged behind the CD player, he pressed it forward. Hard! The mounting snapped. One forceful jerk and the player popped from the dashboard like a new born baby from his mom's tummy. Hurriedly Kerbs cut the wires.

'Don't just stand there watching me, you should check to make sure nobody's coming,' he said.

But I couldn't help it; one ought to learn how to do this kind of thing. You never know when you might need the knowledge and skills. (Outcomes based education turning around to bite the community in the ass.)

Kerbs started on the speakers. After a while he said, 'No, shit, I'm not going to hassle with this, it'll take a lifetime.'

'Okay.' I shrugged. 'O yeah, check out the cubby-hole. The sunglasses . . .'

Kerbs removed my mom's Police sunglasses and stuffed them in his pocket.

'I also planted her cell phone in there. My mom sometimes forgets it in the car. She'll never know it was me.'

It was a Nokia. Small technological wonder: GPS system, WAP enabled (unlike its user) and it could take photos, record sound, you name it. She uses it to phone people.

'Okay, do you have everything?'

'Yes.' Kerbs stuffed the loot into a black

gym bag.

'Alright then, you have to go now.'

'See you later, bru.' Kerbs gave me a pat on the back. 'Open the gate.'

Again, he slipped through the gate. The rain came down even harder now. I watched the raindrops run down the BMW's leather seats.

So much for the new car smell.

Kerbs' car pulled away in the street. It backfired once, sounding like a gunshot.

I entered the house. Everything was dark, but I knew the way to my room. Hey, I must have done it a million times, after long, drunk nights on the street.

The sudden voice from the living room startled me.

'Chris.'

'Dad?' I asked when I saw his silhouette moving against the curtains with the patio light on in the background.

My heart started racing.

'Why didn't you tell us you were going out?'

Two things he said totally confused me.

Numba one: who were the 'us' he was referring to? Was it him and my mother? They haven't been much of an 'us' for a long time now.

Numba two: did he really think I went out? Did or didn't he know?

What could he have heard? What could he have seen?

Silently I rewound the night's events in my mind.

Noises: the click of the opening gate; our voices in the driveway; the brick sending the car's window to hell; the cracking of the dashboard; the click of the gate opening up a second time; Kerbs' car backfiring.

See: fuck all from the house – there were way too many plants. Except if he came out of the house. Kerbs was right, I shouldn't have checked him out, I should have kept an eye out for nosy onlookers.

Fast forward to where we were last.

I realised that it was one of those soapie moments where the silence lasts a lifetime and one of the actors simply tilts his head to the side until it becomes time for an ad break.

Where was my ad break?

Okay, time to decide.

He didn't know – ride the wave.

'I was only out for a while. I didn't think you would mind.'

'You and Kerbs?'

Damn, does he know?

Again, I pulled a soapie response. 'Kerbs?' Testing the water.

'I heard his car backfire.'

Never, bru, where do grown-ups learn these things? He was playing cat and mouse with me. Did he want me to come up with the whole bag of stolen goods?

'Switch on the light so that I can see you.'

Pros & cons, I thought instantly. Con: he might see that I'm lying. Pro: I could see if he doesn't really know.

The light was blindingly bright – like D-day.

We both twitched our eyes until we were used to the light.

I saw the glass of whiskey I had poured for him earlier. He hadn't drunk it. He must have known something was up when I brought him a drink without him asking for it.

He sat there with a full glass in his hands. (That time of night?) Obviously, he was smashed. His shirt was unbuttoned and wrinkled.

He wasn't wearing pants.

I darted off to my room.

Lock the door! Lock the fucking door!

One of these days I am going to smash his skull in, I decided.

I knew he was standing on the other side of the door.

And the voices in my mind came rushing fast and furious.

Lessons on stop streets and how things work in the movies

There was this man who once drove over a stop street at a helluva speed. Next thing he knew: flashing lights, screaming alarms. A traffic cop had managed to chase him down and stop him. (At that time he had already skipped a few stop streets.)

'Hey, what the hell do you think you're doing?' the traffic cop yelled at the guy. 'You ran a stop street back there! Why the fuck didn't you stop?'

The guy checked out the traffic cop and said: 'I don't believe everything I read.'

Ha, ha, ha :-)

MindF**k

And you shouldn't either.

Do you really think my dad sat there without his pants? This is not what this story is about. Leave that for the newspapers. (I don't even know why kids would allow stuff like that to happen to them. They obviously don't know what sharp knives are for.)

Sorry I lied to you about the pants-thing. I was just kinda looking for an excuse to get out of the living room and I didn't want you to think that I'm a jackass. My dad has been keeping his pants on for years now. I think he only took them off twice in his life. The first time being when he made Kelly, my sister, and the second time when he made me.

Ha, ha, ha.

If he wanted anything more, he had to keep himself happy – Mom didn't allow him near her with that thing, if you catch my drift. They slept in separate rooms. Threats of a pending divorce had been poisoning the air for a few months now, but they stuck it out 'for the kids'.

Hey, I should tell you about our family. But let's do it in style – like in the movies. Have you noticed how some of them start? While the credits are rolling, the camera slowly moves across a room (let's say it's some little fuck-faced brother's room). First, you notice a few pics on the dressing table, and then you think: Oh, would you just look at that, they are the perfect family. Colgate smiles, the works. Then the camera glides across the wall and you think: Oh, would you just look at that, he has a wall, man he's so lucky that he doesn't have to live in a squatter camp like millions of black South Africans. The camera pans to something hanging off the headboard, let say it's a girl's panties, and while you are sitting there in your dirty chair in the darkened cinema you think: Oh, the little fucker is already screwing around. Or he likes wearing women's underwear.

You get the picture?

Alright, here is mine:

At my door: life-size posters of Britney Spears and Christina Aguilera. (Did you spot that lie? What?! Haven't you learnt anything from the stop street story?)

Sorry, let's try that again (take two).

At my door: posters of the White Stripes and My Chemical Romance.

On my desk (read: alternative, user-friendly hoarding zone to stash anything imaginable):

- An empty pizza box

- Empty CD covers

- Loose CDs (mostly pirated copies – have you seen the price of original CDs?)

- Overseas magazines (mostly stolen – have you seen the price of overseas magazines?)

- An empty fish tank (cuz the poor

goldfish died), which then became a snake cage (until the snake died).

Now the camera moves towards my bed. As usual, it looks like a war zone. Underneath my bed you will find the following assorted goodies:

- A flat rugby ball. (There was a time when my dad still had hope for me. The rugby ball is the proof of that, but I decided to hell with this, I will not run around chasing shit.)

- Dirty underwear and sour smelling socks, cuz our maid doesn't believe in cleaning up underneath anything.

- Oh crap, there's that biology book which had Amoeba bitching my head off.

And then there are my prized possessions:

- The porno-mags in the drawer next to my bed. (I suspect that the old man uses them at times to assist with the DIY thing. I once found one of them in a slightly different spot from where I had left it.)

- My computer that I mostly use to play games and surf the porn-sites on the net.

And that's my room.

As you can see, there are no photos of the family, cuz this isn't a damn movie. And everyone in this household isn't happy.

unhappy

I'll just have to tell you about them.

TRACK 03

The story about the three Bs and how I came and fucked everything up

Once upon a time there was a mommy Burns, a daddy Burns and little sister Burns. They all lived in a house in Bloemfontein. Langenhoven Park, to be precise. They were very happy. Like the people you see in the shampoo adverts on the TV.

And then I came along. Covered in fat and dripping blood. Kicking and screaming. Perhaps I already knew back then that being born was a big mistake. I should have stayed where I was. (Exactly where that is, I can't say right now, but I reckon that I'll have the answer in the afterlife, so ask me again on that day.)

I think my birth fucked up everything. Could be because I wasn't exactly planned. It fills one with an overwhelming sense of pride to know that you 'were not planned'. It's almost like being a gatecrasher long before you could remember.

Kerbs says that the best part of me ran down my dad's leg. I reckon he might not be way off mark. I think my dad would agree.

I was a naughty shit as a child. At the age of four, I sunk my pearly whites into one of the girls at the nursery school. There was a lot of blood. It streamed over her arm and dyed her pink, icing sugar-like dress red. My teacher, Miss Gilda, couldn't decide whether she should faint or give me crap. She made these weird noises like I reckon a pig would make if it's being castrated. I was scared shitless; I thought she was going to die. Stricken with fright I sank my baby teeth into the tender skin just below her knee. I bit down hard. Only then did she shut-up.

Miss Gilda and the icing sugar girl both had to go for tetanus injections. My mom couldn't believe that I would do something like that. After all, she had always taught me that one should never bite other people. I was asked to leave the school. From then on I stayed with our maid, Anna.

Anna didn't understand a word of English. At the age of five, I decided to teach her. And I'm proud to say that all my hard work wasn't in vain – she still swears like a Gautenger stuck in a traffic jam.

My sister is one year older than I am. Nineteen. At first, she was the model child, getting distinctions in all her subjects, until grade 9. Then she decided: what the fuck. And she threw open her legs. Fourteen boyfriends, two shiners and one abortion later, she doesn't take any shit from my parents either.

Last year, Kelly finished Matric. She said there was nothing to it. You basically have to be a moron to flunk your Matric these days. The Department of Education tries really hard not to disappoint the learners. And just in case things didn't go according to plan, she informed the principal that her great-grandmother was black. This meant Kelly was historically disadvantaged and they had to try harder to pass her at the end of the year. And they did.

Kelly now works at a pizza place and she mostly smells of dough and melted cheese.

My mom and dad are like a see-saw. When one is at the bottom, the other is on top. And when one is on top, the other one is at the bottom. I'm not talking about sex here; I'm talking about their jobs.

My dad was an estate agent. Things went well for him; he even ranked as top seller a few times at Aïda. The pay was good, but not enough. Then he decided to start his own estate agency. People probably didn't find it amusing buying a house from a place called 'Burns Housing'. Needless to say, the place folded like a fortune cookie.

Then he gave the corporate thing a shot and went to work at the bank. Saambou. A few years later, all the personnel from Saambou were sacked. Everyone heard the rumours, but nobody wanted to believe it. Finding a job after that was a bitch. Affirmative action and the pale-male-syndrome closed all the doors.

And then came the back breaker.

My mom, who worked as a personal assistant at an investment firm, had in the mean time gradually started climbing the corporate ladder. In the evenings she studied so hard you could almost see the Unisa books flying. And during the day she attended every imaginable conference and sucked up to all the bosses. And before we knew it, her pay check was bigger than my dad's.

It was a recipe for disaster. Their marriage went down the drain. No man's self esteem can handle things like that with grace.

He grabbed at straws and tried selling funeral policies to keep his dignity. She just kept on earning more and more in bonuses each month. She bought a BMW. He had to downgrade to a second-hand Mazda.

But they stayed together under one roof, in separate rooms. Kelly and I could see the way they looked at each other. And we knew: the shit had hit the fan.

Oh, my car, my car

Saturday morning.

SMS to Kerbs:

> my mom just gave a
> helluva scream. i think
> she saw her car :-[

It was the first time in months that Kelly was home on a Saturday morning. Did her boyfriend dump her? Well, good for him! Normally she dumped the boyfriends long before their sell-by date. It made her believe she had the power to end it all. It gave her a false sense of security. And it thankfully stopped those tear-filled sessions that could last for days afterwards.

I checked her out as she walked from the kitchen cupboard to the fridge. Tried to see if anything was wrong. Waiting for that you-men-are-all-lower-than-swine-shit outburst. Maybe a tear.

She kept a straight face. Then perhaps everything was still a-okay between her and the boyfriend. (What's his name again? Something like Cutlet, Cunter, Gutter? Gunter? Never mind.)

'They broke into mom's car last night,' Kelly said when she noticed me watching her.

'Oh?'

What was I supposed to say? Ask her about the car? Who cares, I was there, wasn't I?

Kelly emptied some Rice Krispies in a bowl, then cold milk and three spoons of sugar. I shuddered at the thought of the cold milk. And the food. I don't know how people can have breakfast. I'd rather have a cigarette.

I watched her taking the first mouthful of cereal, heard the snap-crackle-pop. A stream of milk ran down her chin. She wiped it off with her hand and took a second bite, this time smaller. I imagined hearing the sugar crunching underneath her teeth, how it glided down her throat only to appear days later as a cellulite dimple on her white butt-cheek. And I could see the three cartoon-characters on the cereal box laughing at her.

'What are you looking at?' she asked after a while.

I just grinned, wondering if I should tell her: I'm watching you fattening yourself up. But I just left it. That was a war for another day.

I heard someone at the front door. A while later my dad stepped into the kitchen.

'The car's window was smashed. The radio is stolen,' he said.

'I know.'

'Oh, you do?' he asked.

Same tone as last night. That well-buddy-I-know-too-tone of voice. But did he really know, or was it my imagination?

'Kelly told me.'

'Ah.' He scratched his stubbly beard and sat down next to Kelly.

'I'm going to check it out,' I said, to get out from under my dad's eyes. I knew he watched me disappearing into the hallway.

I stepped outside barefoot, only dressed in jeans. No shirt.

My mom was sitting in her car. The look on her face like someone mourning a loved one.

'Fuck, Mom, I heard they –'

'Please stop cursing,' she snapped, not even looking my way. Her hands were clamped around the steering wheel, her eyes staring intently through the windscreen.

'Mom, didn't you park the car inside?'

'Does it look like I did?'

I walked around to the passenger's side. The leather was still wet after the rain. The carpet too. Pieces of glass everywhere. My eye caught the screwdriver on the carpet. Shit, it was the one that Kerbs used to lift out the CD player. I picked it up quickly. Mom's eyes flashed towards me.

'Don't touch it!'

'Sorry.' I shrugged my shoulders, but I didn't drop the thing. 'The police won't go through too much trouble anyway. Fingerprinting and the like, I mean.' I'm hoping, actually. 'They'll want to know if you have insurance, you answer 'yes', case closed. They've got bigger worries than stolen radios.'

'My sunglasses are missing too.'

'They've got bigger worries than stolen radios and sunglasses.'

My mom looked so sad sitting there. Her blond hair was still messed up from the sleep. Her eyes looked tired. She still looked a bit befuddled. Maybe it was from the two sleeping pills. Or maybe it was just the sadness for the car. I think she loved it more than she loved my dad. She probably got better service from the car.

'I should go back in,' she said. 'I have to phone PG Glass. Find out when they're opening.'

As soon as she left, I wiped the screwdriver clean. Just in case.

Then I stepped back into the house.

I heard my mom looking for her cell phone.

The Mystic Boer

It was Saturday night. Kerbs and I were on our second beer. We were at the Mystic Boer in Kellner Street. The place was jam packed. Bodies rubbing up against each other. One of Muse's songs was playing. I tried figuring out which one it was, but the name eluded me. I saw Kerb's leg moving with the beat of the music. He probably didn't even notice it; he only checked out the girls strolling past to the restroom, the bar or on their way outside.

We slouched on the red couch in front of the wall with the silver corrugated iron sheet. Nice spot. Close to the bar. Further off guys were playing pool. Every once in a while you could hear the crack of the pool balls over the music. The Voortrekker lads on the wall at the back stood watch over us. I sometimes wondered what they would have done if they were here now. Would they have joined us for a beer? They looked so emaciated; maybe they'd rather like a slice of Mystic pizza.

Sky Eyes found us in the dusky club. Sky is my other buddy. If you're a girl and you had to choose between myself, Kerbs and Sky, you would probably choose Sky. He's the most presentable of the three of us. Someone you could introduce to your mother. And he has the looks – blond hair, blue eyes. It's weird that he's still single.

'I almost floored a car watch just now,' said Sky, sinking down on the couch next to me. 'Fucking old timer tells me that I shouldn't drink too hard.'

Kerbs and I laughed, but we knew that was all talk. Sky wouldn't do something like that. He has a soft heart.

'Did you tell him you only drink Red Bull? To give you wings!'

'Fuck you.' Sky got up. 'I'm gonna get a beer.' He ambled over to the bar.

Sky tried getting one of the barmen's attention. Eyes cast down they scrambled from the Coke machine, over to the booze bottles, to the till. Only then did they make eye contact with another customer.

A poster was stuck to one of the walls of Mystic:

MindFuck

The biggest rock festival ever to hit the Free State!
Three days of music and madness!

• Arno Carstens • Karen Zoid • Prime Circle
• 16 Stitch • Wonderboom • Koos Kombuis
• Kobus! • The Parlotones • And many more ...

Are you ready to fuck with your mind?
Get into the mosh pit!
Allemanskraal Dam • 4-6 February

And that was where we were going. What we needed cash for. Why Kerbs and I broke into my mom's car.

Kerbs was going to sell off the stuff. He had his contacts for scaly ventures like that. They wouldn't screw him over.

'I've done this kinda thing a million times, bru, don't worry.'

But somehow I was still worried. What if things went wrong?

Sky Eyes came back with his beer.

'Hey, fuck, where's ours?'

'Get your own. Do I look like a beer brewery?' Again, he fell down between us.

'All right,' said Kerbs. 'I'll get my own. I don't even drink that crap. I drink Black Label and piss Castle.'

Kerbs wanted to demonstrate and almost fell of the couch. Not only was he drunk, but he was high as well. Sky and I laughed as he tried straightening up only to lose his balance. Sky gave him a kick on the ass and he stumbled onward to the bar.

'How're things moneywise for you, Sky?' I asked when Kerbs left.

Sky had to provide for himself. The radio and other stuff only covered my and Kerbs' MindFuck expenses.

'I'll come up with the money, no worries. My old-timer will provide, as always.'

Sky was a lucky son of bitch. I reckoned his parents stuffed him with the money just so that he would stay the hell away from home. Even though he was more presentable than Kerbs or me, he remained a social embarrassment for his parents. As soon as he finished Matric that year, there would already be a flat nearby the university standing at the ready for him. No worries anymore for his mommy and daddy, because he would be out of their house and out of sight permanently. (Then we are going to party like there's no tomorrow.)

'I'll bring the meat. And beer,' said Sky.

'Will they let us in with beer? Don't you have to buy it there?'

'Shit, I hope not. We'll take some along just in case.'

'And some reefer.'

Sky started smiling. 'It's going to be an insane party, Burns.'

Then I noticed Sky's smile disappearing in an instant. It was as if his face went numb. Shit, no, not here. Not now. His eyes turned inwards. His body started shaking. The beer bottle slipped from his hand and rolled across the floor.

'Kerbs!' I shouted over the noise of the people and the music. 'Fuck, Kerbs!'

The people crowded around us. Kerbs broke through them.

Sky lay on the floor. His body shook. I held him down. Kerbs grabbed his head, opened up his mouth. Pressed down his tongue.

'Is he alright? Should we get a doctor?' someone asked.

'No, he'll be fine,' said Kerbs.

'Sky, can you hear me?' I asked.

He didn't answer me.

His shuddering body calmed down.

Like spent waves subsiding after crashing on the beach.

His eyes slowly opened up. I got frightened when I saw the terror filled look in his eyes. And I knew it had happened again.

It wasn't just an attack. There was something else.

We helped Sky straighten up. He rubbed his face. His neck. He still looked a bit dazed, a bit off balance. I wrapped my arm around his neck to keep him on his feet. He touched the back of his trousers. They were wet. From the beer on the floor, I hoped.

The nosy crowd moved away, talking, turning around a few times to catch a final glimpse of us.

'Let's just fuck off,' said Sky. We passed through the people. Sky opened and closed his mouth, as if tasting something bitter on his tongue. Then he said: 'Shit, Kerbs, when did you last wash your hands?'

The things that Sky says sometimes frighten people

It was Tuesday. Kerbs, Sky and I were in Mimosa Mall. Kerbs only came along to check out the girls' tits. Bloem has some lovely girls. And the lovely girls have even lovelier tits. Kerbs had a keen eye for things like these and he wasn't ashamed of expressing his admiration.

'You're going to smack right into a trashcan or something if you keep staring around like that,' Sky said to Kerbs.

'Yeah, or tumble over a railing somewhere,' I added.

Sky laughed. He also knew that anything

was possible with Kerbs.

'Every sport has its injuries,' Kerbs just grinned.

We strolled around for a while on the ground floor of the mall and then took the escalator to the first floor, past Exclusive Books, straight to Musica with its industrial look. Immediately, someone approached us, a black girl.

'Can I help you with anything?'

'Yes, a blowjob,' Kerbs tuned her. She quickly marched off, furious.

'Fuck, Kerbs, why do you say things like that?' I asked.

Kerbs shrugged. 'What does she know about Green Day, anyway?'

I noticed her keeping an eye on us. I was used to that. Places like these always have their scallywag scouts. Come to think of it, everywhere you go, there are people watching you – some of them without you even knowing it. Like in a movie theatre. You think you're sitting there in the dark and nobody can see you, but you are wrong, my bru. They keep their eyes on you even in the dark. Check it out next time you're at the movies. There's always a little red light shining, up on the ceiling. It's a camera, and it's watching you munching your popcorn and gulping down your Coke. Every single move you make . . .

Sky found the Green Day CD which he came for. 21st Century Breakdown.

'Are you going to listen to it first?'

'Of course. It's too bloody expensive to just buy it. Did you notice, Burns? When the rand was so weak a few years ago, the price of CDs skyrocketed. And when the rand got stronger, the prices stayed the same. Somewhere there's a fucker pocketing our money. And they think we don't know it."

'Shit, Sky, you should just download the stuff from the internet, man. Much cheaper,'

I said while flipping through a stack of Pink
Floyd CDs. (Classic stuff.)

'No, hell, I want the originals.' Sky
made his way to the counter. 'Can I listen to
this?' He gave the CD to the guy behind the
counter, who removed the sticky tape from
the sides. (Can you fucking believe it – the
store tries stopping theft with sticky tape?)

Sky put the headphones on. I shuddered,
thinking of the millions of crawling head
lice, other people's filthy oily ears and the
things that might have already started
living on those headphones. Gross!

Kerbs came sauntering closer. 'I'll wait
outside,' he said. 'Don't take forever.'

Sky pressed the volume button on the
counter to max. I knew why. The shitty rap
music that played in the store was so loud
that you could barely hear the music in the
headphones.

Sky pressed the next track button.

He listened for a while. Then suddenly he removed the headphones.

'We shouldn't go anymore,' he said.

'What? What are you talking about?'

'MindFuck. We should stay away.' He looked scared.

'Why?' I asked cautiously. And as soon as I said it I knew that I should have kept my mouth shut.

'I saw blood. The other night in Mystic. You know, when . . .'

'Yes . . .'

'Blood, Burns. Bad shit is gonna happen if we go.'

'Fuck, Sky, why are you telling me this? I hate it when you come up with this crap.'

He put the headphones back on again. Chose the next track. But he was still looking at me. With those blue eyes that could see things before they happened. His Sky Eyes.

And he looked concerned. Fucking concerned.

An alarm suddenly went off at the store entrance. Sky and I both swung around. We knew it was Kerbs.

TRACK 07

Dreams, blood and money

'Blood, Burns,' said Sky in my dream that night. We were floating in a boat on the water. I couldn't see the land at all. I somehow knew it was out there, but I just couldn't see it. I heard music rolling in from far away. I think it was 'Night falls like a grand piano' by Wonderboom.

'Blood, Burns,' Sky repeated, lifting his arms, his palms facing up. He extended his hands to me. The stretched skin turned pale and then blood slowly started oozing to the surface. It formed a small arch in the palm of his hand. He turned his hand over. The blood dripped into the boat.

Drip, drip, drip.

The red lines ran down against the Perspex inside of the boat.

'What are you doing?' I asked.

'I'm performing magic,' Sky said.

'What kinda magic?'

'Mind magic. And you're my volunteer.'

I didn't know what he meant. In a way it probably made sense. No, it meant nothing. Sky couldn't do magic. I wanted to ask him what he meant, but something stopped me. Perhaps it was his eyes that had suddenly turned black. Like black holes one should stay away from.

'Where's Kerbs?' I asked.

'He's getting rid of her. Making sure that they don't find her.'

'Who?'

'You know.'

Sky pointed to the water with a bloody finger. A drop of blood ran down the shaft of his finger, clinging to the tip for a while and then dropping into the pitch-black water.

The water became clear.

I saw Kerbs' face staring up from out of the water.

He laughed at me.

Then it seemed as if he wanted to tell me something. I held my ear closer to the water to listen. His arms suddenly shot out, grabbing my head and pulling me from the boat.

The water was deadly cold. Kerbs' fingers pressed hard against my temples, his legs intertwining with mine. I tried kicking to get to the surface. It didn't help. Kerbs was amazingly strong. I was running out of breath. I tried freeing myself from his grip. I thought I heard him laughing. It was a weird sound, like a dog being run over. We sank even deeper. My heart stopped . . .

And I knew that somewhere there was land. Even though I couldn't see it.

I knew it was only a dream.

Everything.

Sky couldn't perform magic.

'Dude, fuck Sky. I'm fed up with his Nostradamus-shit.'

I was in Kerbs' flat. A pigsty of dirty dishes, dirty underwear, dirty everything. It didn't bother him at all. He said that someday he would bang a girl real good and then ask her to clean up his place. Sort of as compensation. Yeah right, as if that's ever going to happen, but that's the way Kerbs' mind operated. He lived in a world of his own, like an ant on a sugar high inside a sugar pot.

Kerbs sat opposite me on the bed, his back against the wall. He took another sip of his beer. I told him what Sky had said. But I kept my mouth shut about my dream. He didn't like that sort of thing. Neither did I. I hated it when people told me about their dreams. As if it had some or other deeper meaning.

I don't believe in dreams.

But why did this one concern me so much?

'If he wants to stay, let him. We'll manage fine without him. Check this out, I got the money.' He removed a roll of money from his pocket.

'How much?'

'Seven hundred bucks.'

'Is that enough?'

'Who knows? By the way, I hope you don't mind. I gave your ID number to the guys at the pawn shop.'

It was like a brick hitting you in the nuts. 'My what?!'

'You're in this thing too, aren't you?'

'Yes, but . . . Shit, Kerbs, how could you do that? And how do you know my ID number?'

'You shouldn't leave your stuff lying around.'

'If I get into shit, Kerbs, I'll rat you out.'

'Come on, buddy, that's not the way things work. Guys like us – we cover for each other.' He fell back on the bed again. He had a dodgy grin on his pie-hole. He knew just which buttons to push. He pressed the beer bottle against his lips, but didn't drink. 'I pawned that CD I stole as well. Bad vibes.'

'How did you get past security?'

'Ways and means, brother.'

TRACK 08

Make like a tree and leave

'Are you in or out?' Kerbs asked Friday morning.

Sky seemed uncomfortable.

'In or out?' Kerbs repeated.

'I'm just saying: we should be careful.'

'Careful about what, Sky?' I could see Kerbs was irritated. He jammed more stuff into the boot of the car.

'I don't know! Okay?'

'Well I know. You should learn to relax

more. You take life far too seriously. This weekend we're going to party like the fucking world is going to end.'

Sky shrugged his shoulders.

'So, are you gonna chicken out, Sky?'

Sky stared at me. I'd made my decision. I was going. It was the weekend. I wasn't going to sit at home and watch TV just because Sky saw some blood.

'I'm coming with.'

'What are we waiting for then?'

We had to take my dad's car. Kerbs' car was broken. He explained precisely what the problem was, but what did I care. That old piece of metal with the flames on the sides was in any case only a coffin with flash rims and Firestone tyres.

Kerbs decided that we should blow the dust of my dad's speakers. He turned the volume way up. System of a Down's

'Steal This Album.' (And he had obliged as requested.)

I leaned forward and set it softer. 'I can't hear myself think.'

'You shouldn't think. You should feel.' He turned it up again.

Sky laid stretched out on backseat. How he could sleep through all the noise, only he knew. He said he needed to get his beauty sleep for the night.

Kerbs lit a joint. He took a deep puff and holding it in, he passed the joint on to me. The sweet aroma oozed through my body. How they could ban this stuff was beyond me. I mean, why should all the good stuff be banned? Should life remain shitty? Are we meant to be confronted with Riaan Cruywagen's wig every second night while he tells us how corrupt the world is? Why don't they ban the boring stuff?

Politicians, for example. That boring lot of assholes that only steel our money and still want us to vote for them every few years. But I won't vote for somebody just because he stuck his fucking mug shot onto every streetlight in our neighbourhood. That, by the way, is also the only time you see them in the neighbourhood, up on the lampposts during elections. Man, those fuckers can't even see to it that those bloody posters are removed after the elections – how are they going to run a country? Especially this country with its political correctness whenever it suits.

I say ban politicians.

And while you are at it, also ban taxis, Morning Live, women's magazines, Teletubbies, traffic cops, Matric, newspapers, crappy 'but wait there's more' adverts, cyclists, ah fuck, every pathetic shitless thing that is doomed to hopeless failure.

'Stop!' Kerbs shouted over the music.

My colon nearly knotted with fright. I slammed on the brake, almost ramming it through the floor. The car skidded across the road and came to a halt.

Even Sky jumped up on the backseat.

'What the fuck?'

'Reverse!' shouted Kerbs.

'What the fuck?' Sky repeated.

We all stared back.

'Give her a lift. She's also going to MindFuck. Check out her cardboard sign.'

We were on the N1. The small town of Winburg was on our right-hand side. Under the off ramp stood a girl. Black hair. Skinny, with nice tits. And she needed a lift.

It was like a sum total you couldn't get wrong even if you tried.

$1 + 1 = 2$

Or: $3 + 1 = 4$

As easy as that. No two ways about it. We had to take her with.

'No,' said Sky. 'Leave her.'

'What the fuck?' laughed Kerbs. 'And you're not even high.'

'We'll vote.'

Sky lost, of course.

I drove backwards the hundred metres or so. She had seen us. She grabbed the blue bag at her feet and came running.

Sweet, I thought.

'Can I get a lift?' she asked as Kerbs rolled down the window.

'Hey, I never say no to a nice girl like you. Jump in.'

'Kerbs, where's your manners? Let the girl sit in front,' I said.

Kerbs glared at me. 'You want her all to yourself, ha?'

I smiled. 'Come on, Kerbs. When last did I ask you for something?'

Kerbs got out and climbed in at the back with Sky. I saw him explaining to Sky how big her tits were. He had this look of satisfaction on his face. Sky only shook his head. I got back on the N1 again.

'So, who are you, where are you going?' the girl asked.

'We're going to MindFuck,' I said. 'This is Kerbs, Sky and I'm Burns. And you?'

'I'm Tina. But this weekend you can call me Partygirl.'

'Oo-eei!' Kerbs shouted. 'Partygirl!'

I looked at Partygirl. She was genuinely nice. Cherry-red lips, blue-blue eyes and a skin like vanilla yogurt. She wore jeans and a black T-shirt that read: Fit in or fuck off.

'Aren't you afraid of hiking?'

'No, I always do this. Never had any problems. You're not going to be the first guys to give me problems, are you?'

'No, we'll behave ourselves,' said Kerbs with a devilish smile.

'But I hope not too much,' she laughed. She turned to me. 'Especially not you.' She put her hand on my leg, rubbed a bit higher. I felt myself growing stiff.

'Change the CD,' Sky shouted from the back.

'Where's my bag?' Partygirl asked. Kerbs handed it over from the back. Partygirl ruffled through her things and removed one of the Springbok Nude Girls' CDs. The Fat Lady Sings. 'I want to get Arno Carstens to autograph it for me.' She slipped the CD into the front-loader and skipped to track 2. It was 'Blue Eyes'.

Partygirl closed her eyes as the guitar

started playing. After a while she said: 'I love this song. It's about suicide amongst policemen, did you know?'

I shook my head. Arno's haunting voice filled the car. Even Kerbs fell silent. We simply listened.

Allemanskraal Dam

Just before twelve we turned off to Aldam. We made our way down the curving road, past the trees, and later the big dam wall. As a child of the Free State, for me this was one of the big dams. I only knew Allemanskraal Dam and Erfenis Dam. Erfenis Dam where we went fishing when my grandpa was still alive. Every once in a while we went to Aldam for a weekend or only for the day. I remembered the game reserve where you had to look around damn hard before seeing anything at all. But the animals were there, we were probably just impatient because they didn't line up next to the car so that we could check them out. We are the TV generation. We want everything easy. Why would you want to search for the animals amongst the trees, bushes, grass and rocks?

At Aldam you could also fish, jump trampoline, play put-put, and there were these big swimming pools, the dancing area and the restaurant with the stuffed up animals in the dark hall on the way to the restaurant.

That's what I remembered, but it had been a while since I'd been here. Suddenly the gate I knew from my younger days came into view. (As if I'm so bloody old now.) A large thatch roof covered the road, painted walls stretching out to the sides. There was a large banner extending across the thatch roof: MindFuck Rock Festival.

Kerbs rolled down the window, leaned out and shouted: 'Let's get this party started!'

Partygirl followed his lead. She sat in the open window, arms on the roof. 'Yesss! MindFuuuuck!'

The man at the gate only shook his head. Security, dressed up in a white shirt and black trousers. I stopped next to him.

'Morning, sir,' he said to me.

'Unfortunately sir couldn't join us. He had to stay at home.' Partygirl giggled softly.

Another person appeared from the gate cubicle. He asked for our tickets. The first guard looked in the boot for hidden passengers, and then shot a glance behind the backseat.

'Don't worry, we didn't hide anyone. You're wasting your time,' Partygirl told the guard. The guard only nodded. He took his job very serious.

We all received yellow plastic wristbands.

'Don't remove these. If you don't have one on, you're out. No excuses. And these are the rules. Every party should have rules. Enjoy.'

I took the brochure from him. The other guy handed out plastic bags which read MindFuck on the side, through the window.

I gave them to Partygirl. 'Oh, presents for me.' She passed along Kerb and Sky's bags to them. The red and white boom rose up and I drove through.

'Condoms!' Kerbs yelled as if it was the first time ever he had seen one. He immediately started blowing one up, tied a knot at the end and pinched it in the closed car window, leaving it to flutter about on the outside.

'What else is in there?' I asked.

Partygirl unpacked the stuff on the dashboard:

• six condoms

• a sample of suntan lotion

- a plastic sunscreen from one of the sponsors

- liver pills for tomorrow's hangover

- a small plastic key holder in the form of a brain being bashed in with a hammer

- a Blunt-magazine

- a program with the weekend's happenings

Signs indicated the way to the festival grounds. I followed them, while Partygirl changed the CD. Karen Zoid. Her other favourite, she said, because the girl had balls.

The party was held alongside the dam. From the hill I could see the roof of the stage sticking out. Only one? I thought. No wait, there was another one further off. Probably to ensure that the sounds didn't clash. The second one was smaller. For up and coming bands seeking exposure, Partygirl read in the program.

'Tomorrow morning there's an open mike session for anyone interested in seeing what it's like to be a rock star.'

Kerbs rammed Sky in the ribs. 'Hey, we have to go.' Sky only sat there like a wet panty.

'I'll join you, Kerbs,' Partygirl said above Karen Zoid's voice. She sat back to front on the seat, with the program still in her hand. 'They supply the band, all you have to do is sing. It'll be a blast!'

'I want to smash a guitar to pieces,' Kerbs said.

In the rear-view mirror I saw a smile creep across Sky's face. And I saw Kerbs checking out Partygirl. Without thinking, I placed my hand on her leg. She glanced at me furtively but didn't remove my hand.

We made our way down the steep tar road towards the dam. Slowly, because there were speed bumps. We passed the caravan park. There were open spots set out but few people had started using them at that time. We were going to try and find a place near the water. That's where things were going to happen.

A gravel road appeared before us. Alongside it there were large trees towering above stretches of tall grass. Where the trees ended the ground was covered with fine grass. It was here where the music stages and the ramps for the BMX and FMX competitions were set up. A large area was demarcated, reaching up to the water's edge – the place where the tent town started growing. There were already a crapload of cars. And guys and girls in different stages of undressing.

'Stop,' said Kerbs. 'I'll find us a nice possie. It'll be easier than driving around looking for a spot.'

Sky got out with Kerbs. Partygirl and I watched as they disappeared amongst the people, cars and tents. Already there was music coming from the main stage. I didn't know the band. Probably new to the scene.

Partygirl and I were alone in the car. She looked at me as if expecting me to say something. One of those uncomfortable silences. But inside my head there was a blaring noise. She was so damn hot. I stared at her body underneath the black T-shirt and I longed to slip it off her. I wanted to touch her naked skin. Caress her naked breasts. Watch as her nipples got hard. Kiss her on . . .

'All right, guys, follow me!' Kerbs shouted.

Fuck, just when I started getting excited.

Kerbs ran out ahead of the car. I followed him slowly, carefully trying not to drive over the tents that had already been set up.

It was truly a nice spot Kerbs and Sky had chosen. Ten steps away from the water. A bit damp, but it was okay. That was where we'd settle down for a kickass weekend.

I got out of the car and made my way down to the water to stretch my legs.

The dam's waves rippled and broke continuously against the shore. A small bird waded around looking for food in the shallow water, not at all bothered by all the people. Further away, a large, black bird stretched its wings, gliding across the water. On the other shore some animals – cows perhaps – roamed on the lime green grass.

I turned around when I heard unfamiliar voices behind me. It was the guys in the tent next to us saying hallo.

'Where are you oukes from?'

'Bloemfontein,' I said.

'And Winburg,' Partygirl added.

The guy with the dreads frowned. He didn't have a clue where Winburg was. 'We're from Jo'burg.'

Fuck, huh, I thought, and what's that to me? But they looked like a nice bunch of dudes. Later on I saw a few girls hanging around with them.

Sky started unpacking the stuff from the boot. I noticed that he wasn't himself. He hadn't talked much during the journey. He removed the tent, which I had borrowed from the neighbours (without them knowing about it). The cooler bags, tog bags and other various shit followed.

'Are you okay?' I asked him when Kerbs started setting up the tent.

He shrugged his shoulders.

I didn't enquire any further. My cell phone rang. It was my dad, I saw on the screen. I didn't bother answering. I knew what he wanted.

I closed the car's boot and went to help Kerbs with the tent.

TRACK 10

Lost souls and their sins

www.sevensins.com says there are seven deadly sins: Pride, Sloth, Anger, Envy, Gluttony, Lust and Greed. You can recite it like a rhyme; almost spit it out like Minora blades.

I reckon that I was one of Generation X's lost souls. For us there were only six sins. Pride had hit the road. Fucking emigrated to Iceland. Of what could we be excessively proud? Our excellent marks in school? Mommy and Daddy? Our country? Ourselves? Fuck, no.

Apparently, pride is the sin out of which all the other sins originate.

But for Generation X it is Anger. Because we don't get what we want. And if we somehow do manage to get it, it isn't enough. We are pissed off because grown-ups don't just fucking leave us alone to go ahead and do whatever we want to, like doing fuck-all for hours. No, we don't want to take out the trash. Also not mow the lawn or clean up our rooms. We want what other people have. And lots of it. (Only the nice stuff, not their shit.) And we want the sinful pleasures that lie in others' bodies. And if we don't get it, we go look for it in ourselves.

And in the end, only the emptiness remains. Nothing takes this away. Not cases full of beer, not ecstasy, coke, heroin, sex, music where someone screams his lungs out in frustration, not laying around and doing nothing, not computer games, dancing, moshing, slamming doors, weird clothes, Nike labels, trendy shoes, CD players, DVDs, ah, fucking name it.

Sometimes we only have to bleed to see if we are still alive. Because we have become black holes. And nobody would miss us if we weren't there anymore.

And so we continue downing cases full of beer, popping ecstasy, sniffing coke, shooting heroin, having sex, listening to music where someone screams his lungs out in frustration, sitting around doing nothing, playing computer games, dancing, moshing, slamming doors, wearing weird clothes, hanging Nike labels around ourselves, buying trendy shoes, switching on CD players, watching DVDs.

———

Seeing that we gave her a ride, Partygirl just assumed that she could stay with us. And it was okay, she was really nice. (Flashback to the scene in the car when we picked her up: Partygirl laughing, saying, 'Especially not you', her hand on my leg, my heart racing.)

The six-man tent had enough room for all of us. Partygirl had her own sleeping bag. And some food. We had a cooler bag with some meat for our braai later, and another cooler bag for beer.

My cell phone rang about four times in a row. It was my dad each time. I didn't answer, I only pushed the reject call button.

'I'm gonna check out the FMX warm-ups, who's coming with?' asked Kerbs.

Partygirl and I went along, Sky wanted to get a nap. He still didn't look well, but I wasn't going to let him spoil my entire weekend.

We walked past the hundreds of tents that were already erected, still becoming even more, past the medics' tent, a beer tent further away and next to that a huge marquee tent from which house music was pumping, to the ramps where a guy on a motocross bike shot up against a steep incline. He went flying through the air, one hand on the handlebars, the other on the seat with his body hovering centimetres above the bike in the air and his legs pointed backwards. The Superman Seat Grab. His timing was perfect.

While the next rider was getting ready Partygirl glanced at me. She smiled and took my hand. And later, when Sick Nick did a Helicopter, she gently slipped her hand in underneath my T-shirt, around my body. And then she softly started telling me why she really came there.

TRACK 11

Sky's next revelation

When I went back to the tent to get another beer, I found Sky lying on a foldable mattress. Curled up and fast asleep. There is always this one asshole amongst a group of people whenever you go out. The guy pissing on the fire.

Ah, just let him be, it's his own money he is wasting. Softly I opened up the cooler box and removed three beers. Ice cold. There was a slight movement underneath Sky's eyelids. Was he awake?

Beep-beep, my cell phone went off.

1 message received.

It was my dad. Now he'd started SMSing!

> chris, wheres my car? im going to kill you when you get home. phone me

Yeah, sure.

Delete.

'What are you guys up to?'

I nearly shit myself. I forgot Sky was still in the tent.

'We're checking out the guys on the bikes. It's cool. I think I should steal one and try that myself. I wouldn't want to fuck up my own bike.'

A slight smile tugged at the corner of Sky's mouth. It quickly faded again. He folded his hands behind his head, then again around his body as if he was cold.

'Burns,' he said and kept quiet for a while, only staring at me. Almost through me. I felt a cold chill running down my spine.

'Yes, Sky?'

He inhaled deeply. 'It happened again . . . when you were away . . .'

Oh no, fuck.

I put the beers back in the cooler box and sat down next to him on the ground. 'And? Are you okay?'

Again it went quiet, then: 'One of the girls from next-door helped. She's a nurse. There was a doctor here as well. From the medic's tent.'

'What did he say?'

'Same old shit.'

There was something that Sky wasn't telling me. I saw it in his eyes.

'Sky, what?'

'You don't want to hear it anyway.' He sighed, turned on his back and stared at the roof, where the sun was sinking lower against the canvas. Outside a bunch of girls started screaming and guys whistled.

'Come on, I'm sure you can do better than that!' shouted the guy over the microphone.

They screamed even louder. And then a helluva noise broke loose. The next band had probably hit the stage. Yes, the music started. It sounded like Prime Circle.

'Fuck, tell me.' I shifted around uncomfortably. The hair at the back of my neck stood up. Sky still stared up at the roof.

'That girl we picked up,' he whispered, so softly that I could barely hear. 'She's going to die.'

'Wow, massive revelation, Sky. We're

all going to die. Some time or other.'

'This weekend.'

'What?'

'She's going to die this weekend, Burns . . .'

'How?'

'I don't know.'

'Accident?'

Only then did Sky turn to me. 'I don't know.'

There always has to be one guy in the group who comes and pisses on the fire.

Partygirl organizes the beer

'Let's find the others and go to the main stage,' I said to Sky, just because I didn't know what to say. I took a few beers from the cooler box. 'And then get pissed. Perhaps the Angel of Death will leave us alone if we are motherlessly drunk.'

Sky got up. There was a skull on his wrinkled T-shirt. 'Yeah, whatever, let's go have fun. Maybe I'm just silly.' He put his hand on my shoulder. We went to fetch Kerbs and Partygirl from the FMX show. All around us there were guys and girls who still hung around at the tents, getting really drunk or high.

A guy walked by in front of us, dressed only in a transparent shower curtain. Two holes cut out for his arms and lightly stitched together at the back with fishing line. From the front you could see his dick swinging below the dark bush of hair. 'Fancy a shower?' he asked a girl. She only giggled and moved along.

At another tent there was a braai fire going but the guys had already passed out. They lay across each other, snoring. One of them was sleeping on top of the tent. *Don't piss me off. I don't know where to hide all the bodies anymore*, read his T-shirt.

As we got closer to the ramps we heard the people cheering. 'Give it up for my man, Sick Nick!' More cheers followed.

We found Kerbs and Partygirl amongst the people, watched as one of the bikers did another back flip, and then we were off to the main stage.

Prime Circle was still playing. Ross Learmonth, their main vocalist's voice rocked! Now there was a South African band that was destined to kick butt overseas.

We worked ourselves through to the front, straining past the warm bodies in the crowd. The ground was already covered in beer cans, forcing you to watch your step.

Prime Circle performed another three songs. Partygirl danced as if it was the last band of the weekend. She was already on a vibe. And the sun had only now started touching the horizon. Partygirl raised her hands above her head, grinding her hips she turned to me and took me around the neck. I felt her hips rubbing against me. She brought her face closer to mine, her lips opening slightly as if she wanted to kiss me . . . Then she turned around to the stage again.

'Ladies and gentlemen, Prime Circle!' the presenter shouted. (I didn't recognize him, but I think he was from Kovsie FM.) Cheers, whistles and applause.

'Next up,' the presenter said while the

crew moved around at the back, getting the stage ready for the next band. 'Next up we've got a band that I'm sure you are familiar with. They've supported bands like Simple Minds, Live and The Mission. All the way from Jo'burg. Wonderboom!'

Cheers, whistles and applause.

Partygirl went wild. 'Shit, they're good.' She took another sip of her beer. The foam shook from the can as she jumped up and down.

'And while they set up the stage for Wonderboom, I've got some presents to give away. A big thank you to our sponsor, Castle Lager! Who would like a six-pack of beer?'

Hey, everyone was willing to knock back a few Castles.

'But you're not gonna get it that easily. You'll have to work for it. Now let me see, what can you do to earn this six-pack?'

A couple of morons still tried to grab the

beers from the presenter's hands. Security had to step in.

'Geez, but you oukes are thirsty,' the presenter laughed. He moved over to the other side of the stage, our side. 'Okay, I know. This one is for the girls. Sorry, guys, girls only this time. If you want this six-pack, I want to see some happies, girls. Come on, don't be scared. I won't go and blab on you to your mothers. Any takers?'

'Yes-ss!' Partygirl shouted. She pulled her T-shirt up over her head and her tits jumped out. She threw her arms in the air and turned around for everyone to see.

'Oe-oei-i-i!' I shouted and lifted her onto my shoulders. (Some of the guys around us wanted to start groping.) When Partygirl rose above the crowd they went even wilder.

'There you go! No stopping that girl tonight. Here you are, girl, you've earned it. And a nice rack too. Hell, I wish I could go home with you. With you and my girlfriend.'

Now it was only the guys cheering.

Partygirl jumped up and down on my shoulders. She opened up a beer, spraying the people around us. It ran down my hair. I tilted my head backwards and opened my mouth to drink. Partygirl poured more beer into my mouth.

Kerbs came closer for a sip. Sky only shook his head. 'You're fucking crazy!'

I set Partygirl down on the ground again. She pulled her T-shirt back on, massive smile on her face. 'Don't ever say I don't bring my own booze, boys!' She knocked her can against mine.

TRACK 13

MindFuck and music that makes Partygirl cry

The bands were awesome. By the time the stars came out the party was already scorching hot. Seeing the stars seemed to be a first for the Gautengers, who turned their eyes up in amazement. The city lights had robbed them of the stars all of their lives.

Sweat dripped down our bodies and mixed with the layers of dust covering us. Dust crept in everywhere, our ears, our noses, under our skins. But that was okay. This kind of party only came once a year.

Barney Simon, who had done so much in promoting South African bands, was now the presenter. He tossed MindFuck T-shirts into the crowd and said he'd join us in the mosh pit later on. As a new band set up their gear, somebody started juggling with fire. Mesmerizing ribbons of light illuminated the dark. I could almost imagine it being two fireflies caught in a synchronized dance. (Hell, I was getting lyrical – I must have been in love or something. Or perhaps I was just stoned.)

Even Sky Eyes now seemed more relaxed. I think he'd downed three or more beers earlier, and could now manage fits of laughter from time to time. Or it could just have been the heat.

When 16 Stitch appeared on stage, we began to understand where the word MindFuck came from. It was just another word for head bang. Mosh. Shatter your mind. Jump. Scream. Fuck around. Crash and burn, baby. MindFuck!

All three of us were in the mosh pit – me, Kerbs and Sky. Partygirl also joined us in the deranged mass. Unorganized chaos, like our minds. And somehow it made sense –

crashing into others. Falling down. Getting up and doing it again. It was self-expression without limits. It was a forgotten primeval ritual consuming our minds. Searching for pain that would make us feel human again. Self-sacrifice.

And nothing mattered.

It was just you and the music.

You and your dysfunctional self.

You and your loneliness amongst all of the people.

And the music blasted from the black speakers. We danced, our bodies heating up. Another beer, another spliff, and everything seemed lighter. You forgot everything, like you imagined others have forgotten about you.

The bands changed. Arno Carstens was up next. Partygirl went crazy. She told everybody around her that Arno was her favourite artist. The people didn't seem to give a fuck. You could see it in their eyes. In their distant eyes.

By then bottles and cans littered the ground, making it difficult not to sprain your ankles. Everybody was probably trying to scrub a standing-spot clean for themselves.

The music started up again. Slowly at first, then gaining momentum, faster and faster. Louder. The band members moved under the red lights. Smoke blew across the stage, turning them into ghosts from the land of rock. Arno grabbed the microphone.

Partygirl screamed out loud to the people around her: 'He's singing just for me!'

And through the haze whirling in my mind I thought back to the conversation we'd had earlier at the FMX show. She told me how poor they were. Of her dad's heart attack and his death. The doctor's bills that were piling up. How her mother forced her to leave school. She now worked at the Champion Supermarket in Winburg, sometimes putting away some money to save for a CD without her mother knowing. It was this money she used to pay for the MindFuck ticket. And that morning, when her mother found out about it, she chased Partygirl out of the house. She couldn't ever go back.

Yes, that night Arno was singing only to Partygirl, for she had nothing left but his songs.

As Partygirl stood there, motionless in the midst of the jumping masses, I could see that she was crying.

TRACK 14

The sex scene you've been waiting for (me included)

I took Partygirl back to the tent. She said she wanted to go back while Arno Carstens was still playing. Then it would be as if the music will always be there for her. As if the music would never stop. I don't think I really understood what she meant. My head was spinning and it sounded as if it could have made sense if only I was sober. So I let it go.

Holy shit, there were a lot of tents. Which one was ours? We should've marked it with a light or something. A flashing police light. Fokofpolisiekar – the word dawned on me. What was it? The answer surfaced through my cloudy mind: it was one of the bands that still had to perform. Oh, yes. I wanted to laugh.

'There's the tent,' Partygirl said. She clung to me as we stumbled ahead, falling over tent pegs and empty cans. We stepped in something. What the fuck was that? Did someone take a dump right here between the tents?

The stench followed us all the way to the tent.

'Take off your shoes and leave them outside the door,' I said to Partygirl.

'I think I'd better go and clean them in the water,' she said.

The water?

I thought about my dream. The black water.

'No, take them off and leave them outside.'

'Someone will steal them. I didn't bring another pair.' Her voice seemed tired, laden with a weariness that makes drunken people's voices linger.

She made her way down to the water. Barefoot. Fuck, I hoped there weren't any shards of glass in the mud. Or if there were, that would have been the blood that Sky saw. She waded into the water. I followed her. To clean my shoes as well.

'You're going in too deep,' I said.

Her hips were already below the water's surface.

'Partygirl, get out, please. Come and stand here beside me.'

'The water is fine.'

'Get out.'

'Come in.'

'Fuck, Partygirl.' My voice was anxious.

My heart started beating faster. She went in even deeper.

I tossed my shoes back to the embankment. 'Get out!'

Then I followed her. She kept on walking.

'I think I dropped my shoes,' she said. Her voice echoed clearly from the black water. It sounded weird in the dark.

I'm performing magic, Sky said from my dream. Mind magic. And you're my volunteer.

What did he mean? Mind magic.

'Get out, Partygirl!' The water touched her chin.

I dived forward. The water was icy cold.

'Tina! Stop!' It was the first time that I had called her by her name.

And suddenly she stopped. She turned around. Her face was hidden in the dark. I could only see her forehead and a part of her nose.

'My name is Partygirl.'

'Tina, stop your shit.' As I approached, her face became more visible. My heart relaxed. 'Come,' I said when I reached her.

'I lost my shoes,' she said.

'That's okay, we'll find them. Tomorrow.'

'But by then they'll have drifted away.'

'This is not the sea. It's a dam.'

I didn't know how much sense that made. Are there currents in a dam?

We got out of the water, mud squeezing out from between our toes.

'Let's go find the towels.' Shivering

bodies in the dark. We unzipped the tent. Got in, zipped it back up again. It was warmer inside. She started removing her clothes. I scratched around in my bag for a towel.

'I only brought one.' I held it out to her.

She took it and started drying her body. Her breasts were white, stiff. She dried her long, black hair. I noticed her neck, how it curved off over her shoulders. She unbuttoned her jeans, pulled down the zip, slightly lifting her bum as she pealed the jeans from her legs. She wore white panties. Wet. In front there was a darkened spot.

I stared hypnotized. I could feel myself growing hard, pulled the wet T-shirt over my head and shifted closer to her. I touched her. She looked up. The towel fell in her lap. I caressed her face with the back of my fingers. Her skin was soft. She placed her hand on mine. Gently. She moved my hand down, over her breast, her belly, navel, into the front of her panties. She closed her eyes.

Fuck, I thought.

I felt her heat, wetness.

She unbuttoned my jeans, pulled them down slowly.

She lay down on the wrinkled sleeping bags, pulled me closer.

Without a condom.

She told me that she loved me.

Unwelcome Guest

My body pressed up against Partygirl's. I heard her gasp softly every time I thrust my hips forward.

She wants to talk to me, I thought, but I only had one thing on my mind, and it wasn't talking.

Partygirl was the first to look up. She shoved me off her. The tent's zip opened up.

'May I join the fun?' It was Kerbs.

'No, fuck off, Kerbs. Fuck off!'

'What do you mean?' He reeked of booze. It was too dark in the tent to see his face, but I imagined his pupils being as large as 1 Rand coins. 'Come on, let me have a go at her.'

'No! Fuck off!'

He was kneeling at the entrance of the tent, touching the front of his pants. His hard-on. 'When you're finished, then.'

'No!' Partygirl and I said simultaneously.

'Fuck you, Burns! Then I'll take her!' he hissed through his grinding teeth.

He pushed me out of the way. I rolled over something sharp (a knife?) 'Ouch, shit!'

I felt for blood and saw Kerbs trying to undo his fly, but having difficulty. Partygirl wanted to roll away. Kerbs pinned her down between his knees.

I got up, grabbed Kerbs by the throat, and tried to pull him from her. His dick was hard.

He tore my hands from his throat. Powerfully. Quick. I didn't even see his fist flying; only felt it striking me on the chin, then my temple. The pain shot through my head like a crossbow arrow.

Partygirl screamed.

'Shut up!' shouted Kerbs.

Where's my knife? I felt around between the wrinkled sleeping bags. Kerbs was on top of Partygirl again. His pants down round his knees. His hand over her mouth. Where's the knife? I tossed the sleeping bags aside on a pile, felt around in the darkness. The fucking darkness. I heard Partygirl trying to scream from underneath Kerbs' hand. I saw his crotch starting to push. Shit, no!

'Kerbs!' I yelled. 'Fuck, Kerbs, stop it! You bastard!'

I found what I was looking for. Was it the pocket knife? Short blade . . . No, it was a bottle opener.

'Kerbs!'

I heard him moaning. Voices from outside just passed by the tent.

I was behind Kerbs again, forcing the point of the metal spiral against his back. He knocked me off with his elbow. I shouldn't have gotten so drunk. My arms felt weak. Kerbs was as strong as an ox. He kept on going. Partygirl was crying now.

'Go find Sky,' Kerbs moaned. 'Tell him it's almost his turn.' I remained there, on my knees, my hands burying my face. I didn't want to see, didn't want to hear. 'Go on, fuck, find Sky!'

Sky – the blood that he saw.

Yes, I had to get Sky. He would know what to do. But he had to come quick!

I hurried out of the tent.

Sky was already sitting outside. Waiting his turn?

No, not Sky. He wouldn't have. He was fucked-up, but he wouldn't. Would he?

'Sky?' He looked up. In the distance I heard the music. Lark, I thought, but it didn't matter. Not now. 'Come help, he's raping her. He's fucking raping Partygirl!'

'It's too late,' Sky sighed. 'You know that, Burns.'

'No, come help me!' I grabbed him by the arm, tried pulling him up.

'I told you that bad shit is going to happen.'

'Come on, Sky!'

'Sit. Wait,' said Sky. His voice was calm. Soft. He raised his head and looked up at the stars. As if he could read them. As if tonight's events were written in the stars.

'Fuck, Sky . . .' I was pasted, my body
didn't want to go any further. I felt my
head rushing off in a thousand directions.
I couldn't think clearly anymore. It was the
spliff and booze.

I fell down on the ground next to Sky.

And I wondered: would he go in when
Kerbs had finished?

Kerbs emerged from the tent, crouching.
My first thought was that he looked like
a caveman. Big, hairy, strong. His prey
devoured. I still couldn't see his eyes even
though we were outside. They were just two
dark empty shadows in his head. His mouth
hung slightly open, white teeth flashing.
Like an animal.

He didn't have a shirt on, only an
unfastened pair of pants that he had trouble
buttoning up.

And then I saw his hands.

The blood covering his fingers.

I didn't even have to ask. I just knew. Partygirl was dead.

TRACK 16

Frozen Moment

Blood, was what Sky had said. Blood.

Kerbs saw me staring at his hands. He didn't even try hiding it, putting it away in his pockets or something. He rubbed it, rubbed the blood until it totally covered his hands completely. Like hand cream.

On his face a devilish look. Weird smile. A smirk.

I didn't know him.

I wanted to ask him what the fuck he'd done. But I couldn't. I felt like I was going to implode. I felt like crying. When did I last want to cry? Every day, but I never did. This was different. I had never felt the need to cry for anyone else.

And I wouldn't start now.

Kerbs came and sat down beside me. He put his bloody arm around my neck. 'Buddy,' was all that he said.

Sky shifted around uncomfortably. Did he know how it would all end eventually? Did he know, without saying anything?

Because what had happened was not the end.

Shit like that was never finished.

For a long while now I had stopped paying attention to the music blasting from the stage. I didn't even hear Barney Simon's announcements after each band's performance. I didn't care to see the fire artists. It was as if that moment was frozen in time. And there was nothing, nobody else inside or outside of it.

Just us three. And a tent. And a dead girl inside it.

I didn't know how he'd killed her. Did he snap her neck? (Would there be so much blood if he had?) Or was it a knife? Maybe the bottle opener?

And what did she look like now?

Images of a naked, white body covered with blood smears, entangled hair, staring eyes, gaping mouth, and unnaturally positioned legs, flashed through my mind.

As if I had seen it all before.

But I couldn't see the place where the blood emerged.

'She's fucked,' said Kerbs, again smirking. 'Totally.'

'Why did you do it?'

It was Sky who asked. Who asked what I wanted to.

'Seemed like a good idea at the time.' Kerbs lit up a cigarette, took a drag until the coal glowed brightly, and then blew out a cloud of smoke like a ghost into the night.

'No, Kerbs, why?'

Kerbs took another drag. He watched Sky furtively. 'Because I could.' He said it slowly, every word on its own. Cold chills ran down my spine.

Because he could.

It was enough reason for Kerbs. It always has been.

He lied to people because he could. Stole from people because he could. Ran over dogs in the street because he could.

Enough reason.

Sky and I stared at each other. We didn't know what to say. We wouldn't comfort each other. What would comforting help?

The shit had hit the fan.

'So what now?' I asked.

Kerbs straightened up. 'Now we have to get rid of her,' rasped his voice.

TRACK 17

The plan with Partygirl

'We?' said Sky disgustedly. 'You're the one who did it!'

'We.' There was finality to Kerb's voice. He had already made his decision; he wasn't going to change his mind.

Sky looked at me, wanting advice. Perhaps he was blaming me for not listening when he warned us earlier.

'Come,' said Kerbs. He stood at the entrance to the tent, kept the canvas door closed.

I got up first. Like a zombie. Music

pumped from the stage. Was it . . . ? I couldn't hear clearly. The people screamed and whistled.

Kerbs was like the ringmaster waiting for the circus audience to arrive. He was in control.

I felt Sky's shoulder against my back. Felt my own heart beating, louder than the music.

Kerbs opened the tent.

It was dark inside.

'Go in.' It was an order.

Sky and I bent forward to enter. There was a sweet smell, like blood, but we couldn't see anything. I stepped on something. A foot.

Kerbs zipped up the entrance. He switched on a flashlight. Let the beam play over Partygirl's body, pausing on the dark hair between her legs, then up again, over her naked body. As if proudly showing off his handy work the whole time. As if he wanted to say: look at what I've done. Look at what I'm capable of.

Sky turned his face away.

I wanted to, but I couldn't.

She looked like a doll.

I felt nauseous, swallowed painfully at the sourness that pushed up into my throat.

The blood ran down her face in thin streams, dripping to the floor and following the canvas folds. At places, absorbed by the sleeping bags.

Her face was intact. It was covered in blood but it was intact. It was the back of her head that bled.

And there were blood and hair on the gas cylinder beside her head.

'How are we going to do it?' Kerbs interrupted the silence.

My cell phone beeped twice.

1 message received.

It was my dad again looking for his car, I thought. I didn't have time for him. Not now. But I read the message anyway. It wasn't my dad, it was Kelly.

> wer da hell r u? big shit.
> come home. dad caught
> mom with another guy.
> and he wants his car.

I read the message twice. When it rains, it pours.

I slipped my cell phone back into my pocket.

'We'll put her in the boot of the car and go dump her somewhere,' said Sky.

'Not in my dad's car. He'll kill me if he

finds blood in it,' I said panic-stricken.

'What else then, genius? Do you want to cut her up in pieces and go dump her in some trashcans?'

'We'll bury her.'

Kerbs and Sky only stared at me. As if they were waiting for an explanation.

'We'll cut out the floor and dig a hole under the tent. Nobody will see from the outside. There's enough room in here for a shallow grave's soil.'

I saw Kerbs measuring the space inside the tent with his eyes. He nodded. Sky concurred.

'How will we dig?' asked Kerbs.

'There is a small shovel in the car next to the spare wheel.'

'It will take too long to dig with a small shovel.'

'We have loads of time. There's nothing else we could use. Unless we go and look for something.'

'There's an old VW Beetle close by. It has nice and deep hubcaps; we can dig out a lot of soil with it. I'll fetch it,' said Sky.

Shosaloza

With every shovel full of dirt that fell on the pile, I buried myself deeper. I tried thinking. How did I get there? What was I doing there?

Next to me Sky was busy digging with the hubcap. Kerbs stood outside. On the lookout. When someone approached he tapped on the tent and we stopped working. Until he tapped again.

It was dark inside. We couldn't switch on the flashlight; passersby might see what we were doing inside. Only at times would Kerbs shoot the flashlight over the hole so we could see how we were progressing. Then we plodded on again in the dark.

Partygirl lay at the back of the tent, covered in a sleeping bag. Only one hand showed. Every time Kerbs flicked on the light, her hand caught my attention. The white and red hand against the dark sleeping bag.

On one occasion it looked as if one of her fingers had moved. I got a major fright and dropped the shovel.

'What is it?' asked Sky.

I didn't answer, only touched her hand. It was ice cold.

Sky started digging again.

Somewhere after one o'clock on Saturday morning the music stopped coming from the stage. The dancing tent revived. House music, trance, acid, you name it, it pulsed through the night.

Some guys came back to their tents

with beers in their hands and girls at their sides. Pissed, high, some of them on planets so far-off the Americans haven't even seen them through their telescopes yet.

Kerbs entered the tent. 'Howzit going?'

We couldn't switch on the light. There was too much life in the tents around us, Somebody might have noticed. He climbed into the hole. Probably measured the depth in his head.

'I needed this crap like a hole in the head!' said Sky.

It was quiet for a while and then Kerbs and I burst out laughing. We had to sit down, we laughed so hard. Sky also started. Almost hysterical. From the fatigue and the stress. But mostly the fatigue.

'Hey, bru,' someone tapped against the tent. 'What are you oukes smoking?'

Silence fell like a thunder strike between us.

I went out before the guy decided to enter, a flashlight in my hand. I shone it in his eyes.

'Naught, bru,' he said, closing his eyes. With his hand he tried keeping the light away from his face, all the while standing there swaying, obviously drunk.

I could probably have knocked him over with my finger and he would've stayed down. His T-shirt read: *Is there life after death? Fuck my girlfriend and find out.* (Yeah, right, brother, not tonight. Not in your condition.)

'Are you looking for your tent?'

'Naught, I'm just walking around looking to score a joint.'

'We don't have that shit. Fuck off.' Firmly.

It seemed as if he wanted to continue talking crap. He stepped closer. I looked him straight in the eye.

'Okay, bru, don't be like that. I'm just asking.'

He turned around and walked away. I watched him go, saw him stumbling over a tent peg and totally flattening someone's tent. A guy came creeping out. He wasn't wearing any pants. 'What the hell do you think you're doing?' he screamed and started beating up the drunken dude. A girl stopped him, said that he was a pig.

I got back into the tent.

'Everything all right?' asked Sky.

I nodded.

'Let's continue digging. Kerbs, it's your turn now. Sky, go wait in front of the tent.'

Around half past three that morning we rolled Partygirl into the grave. I made sure the sleeping bag was closed tightly. Kerbs dropped the first shovel of earth on her.

Outside the music was still pumping.

TRACK 19

The party is only starting now, and what are we doing?

At about half past nine on Saturday morning the first signs of life appeared around the camping area. The smell of bacon and eggs frying over early morning fires filled the air.

I had a helluva headache. The smell of the food made me nauseous. I curled myself up smaller on the car's backseat, trying desperately to get some more sleep, but only dozing off for a while before I woke up again.

Sky was sleeping on the front seat. He had been rolling around the whole time. Maybe because of the gear stick poking him in his ribs or because of Partygirl.

Partygirl.

Shit.

What happened to her? Why didn't we just leave her there on the side of the road on the highway?

Damn Kerbs. It was entirely his fault. We should've left him at home. He always screws everything up.

I got up slowly, my whole body tearing apart with pain. Especially my back, from leaning forward whilst digging. I stumbled out of the car to go and take a piss. The plastic toilets were way too far. I found a spot in an empty field where there were fewer tents.

Nothing beats a good piss. You can just stare out into the horizon. And in that watery moment you forget about all your problems. Totally at peace with the world.

While standing there I decided to take a shower as well. I might even feel better afterwards. Then I would go to the medics and find an aspirin. We would probably hit the road in a while. We obviously couldn't stay there the entire time. Not now.

The entire weekend was basically fucked up just because Kerbs couldn't keep his dick in his pants.

I shook off, zipped up and made my way back to the tent. The camping area looked like a whore's handbag. Beer cans, papers, empty meat packs, burnt out fires. Guys and girls passed out in various places.

On one of the tents there hung a black MindFuck T-shirt they'd sold the previous night. Some of them had also been tossed from the stage. I took the T-shirt in passing and stuffed it in the front of my pants. (It will teach that guy to leave his things lying about. Ha, ha, ha.)

Back at our tent I took a sip of water from a bottle. My eyes fell on the raw meat we intended to braai and I quickly flipped the cooler bag closed before I threw up.

I opened up the tent to see what the grave looked like in the daylight.

Kerbs lay sleeping on top of the grave.

I gathered my things together, my towel was still damp from the night before. I made my way over to the place they allocated for the showers.

There was only cold water, but it was okay. I closed my eyes and imagined washing off everything that happened the previous night.

After taking the shower I woke up a medic for an aspirin and then I went back to the tent. There was more life in the camp now. More food smells. Music being played. People talking, cracking jokes, nursing hangovers. Guys bragging about the girls they'd scored with the previous night.

Sky sat across the front seat when I got

there. His shoulder resting against the back of the seat. His feet hanging from the door.

'Let's hit the road,' he said.

I nodded and went to wake Kerbs up.

Everyone around us wanted to know where we were going when we packed up our tent.

'The party has just started.'

I only mumbled something about someone being in the hospital.

Kerbs tossed the tent into the car's boot without folding it up properly. It was now fucked up in any case. He tossed all the other stuff on top of the tent.

I looked at the patch of flat soil. (We'd carried the extra earth out and scattered it about, careful not to leave a bump on the grave.)

If you didn't know what lay buried in

MindF**k

the ground, you wouldn't have suspected anything at all.

Bye, bye, Partygirl.

We drove off.

TRACK 20

Back, as we came

Where to now? We stopped at the crossroad outside Aldam. To our left lay the road to Bloemfontein, to our right the road to Johannesburg, straight on lay Virginia, the old mining town where a slimes dam burst about ten years ago, sweeping away people, cars and houses in Merriespruit. Hell of a disaster.

Like I felt inside at that moment.

Mudslide disaster.

I looked at Sky in the rear-view mirror. He stared down at his hands but obviously knew what I wanted to ask and just said:

'To Bloem.'

I turned left.

I dropped Kerbs off at his flat first, then Sky at his house. Then I drove home. Tired.

I left everything in the car in the driveway and made my way to the front door. It was locked. My key was under the sun dial in the garden. My dad would have freaked out had he discovered that I kept it there, but I wasn't going to carry the thing around with me everywhere I went.

I got the key and unlocked the front door.

Everything was quiet.

I strolled through the house. In the kitchen I grabbed an apple, wiped it clean on my T-shirt and took a bite while sauntering onward.

They had probably gone to town.

I opened my dad's closet in his room. Just to take a look.

The closet was empty. So, he had hit the road. Gone.

For a while I stared at the bare closet but it meant nothing to me. Not then, I was too tired. Maybe it would later.

I fell down on my bed, laying there wearing only my boxers.

I tried sleeping but didn't know if I actually nodded off. I had a pulsing headache. Or was I dreaming I had one?

And was I dreaming when I heard my mom's car coming up the driveway? That she entered the house, stopping at my door, wondering if she should come in? That she touched the handle, pressed it down and released it again without entering? That she walked away?

TRACK 21

Night Ride

I woke up with a start. It was already dark outside. What time is it, I wondered? I couldn't find my watch, looked on my cell phone. Eleven o'clock. I lay quiet for a while, listening for any movement around the house, trying to find out if anyone was awake, but I heard nothing.

There hung an awful stench in my room. Something like the smell of old food. I got up to open a window. I wasn't in the mood to look for the source of the terrible stench.

My mouth felt bitter and dry. I strolled to the bathroom, pissed and gulped down a few sips of water directly from the tap.

The face staring back at me from the mirror didn't look like me. It was pale, had a two day old beard, red eyes and cracked lips.

I felt terrible. The bitter taste was still in my mouth. I pressed out a squirt of toothpaste on my tongue, took another sip of water and rinsed my mouth with toothpaste. My toothbrush was still in my dad's car.

The car. I wondered if it was still there. If my dad had come to fetch it.

I was alone in the house. I made my way to the front door.

The car was still in the driveway. Amazing that he hadn't come to fetch it, I thought. After all the SMSs and voicemails. Perhaps it was because of the thing between him and my mom. And the other man.

The key was still in the ignition. I got in, opened the electronic gate and reversed into the street. The gate closed again. A block further on I remembered that I hadn't locked the house. The front door was probably still wide open. Ah, what the hell.

I drove into town.

I needed a beer. And a spliff.

I drove down Nelson Mandela Drive, past Tempe, the Brandwag Centrum, Mimosa Mall. The street's name changed to Zastron Street. Past the orange and green lights of Stadium Fast Foods (busy as always).

Where should I go? Cool Runnings? Mystic Boer? Maybe to the Waterfront?

But the very thought of all those people crowding those places by now made me realise that I didn't really crave a beer that much. I didn't want to see anyone.

Perhaps I should just cruise through the town centre, I thought. No, not there either. It is a dangerous place at that time of night. Some people don't even go there during the day anymore. I have no idea how all those businesses survive.

To Naval Hill then, I decided. I turned left at the Checkout store on the corner of Zastron and Kloof Street. The traffic light at the old stone church stopped me. I waited. There were no other cars approaching. Should I drive on? No, wait.

Over on the sidewalk I saw someone walking. A girl. In the streetlight I saw she had long black hair, wearing a T-shirt and jeans. She looked around for a moment . . . and my heart stopped.

It was Partygirl!

The traffic light was still red. I shot a glance at the other one to see if it had turned orange already. No, it was still green.

She strode away further and further. It seemed as if she was aiming for a side road. It was dark there.

The light was still red.

Fuck that.

I floored the pedal. The car shot forward.

It was her, I saw as she reached the next streetlight.

Suddenly there were screaming tires behind me. I spotted a white car in the rear-view mirror. How it crashed into the sidewalk. Dust and a honking horn. I probably should've checked if there were any cars coming.

I wasn't going back. No ways.

I was again on the lookout for Partygirl. I found her in Second Street. She walked with her arms folded across her body. I drove closer. Stopped the car, jumped out, leaving the door open.

'Partygirl!'

She glanced over her shoulder at me. I could see that she was scared. She quickened her pace.

It wasn't her.

It wasn't her.

I got back into the car and sat bent forward over the steering wheel. Should I have cried? It was what other people would have done. But I couldn't.

I made a U-turn and turned right at the crossing. I wasn't in the mood for Naval Hill anymore. I was on my way home.

The white car was still parked on the sidewalk in front of the church.

The driver noticed me again. He probably hoped that I'd come back, but I drove past. He gave me the finger. And I returned the favour.

Back through the darkened streets. Past the liquor store, Receiver of Revenue, the blue glass building, and then I saw her again . . .

Partygirl.

The same hope.

The same disappointment.

Peace at last

Kelly hammered on my bedroom door. I'd noticed that she was home but I wasn't in the mood to talk to her. She would only bitch and moan about Mom and Dad and how shit it was that they wanted to separate, and about the other guy who fucked everything up in our household. (As if it weren't fucked up a long time ago.)

Point was – I didn't need it. Not right then.

My mind was muddled and my body felt like an ant farm inhabited by millions of little moving black ants tunnelling through my flesh. Scurrying about, carrying pieces of cut flesh out of me. I could almost feel their small feet tickling in my intestines. And I felt like one of them – I wanted to keep on moving and moving.

I scratched around in my closet until I found a small suitcase. (My old grade 1 bag, could you believe it?) It was where I kept everything my parents weren't supposed to see. They always went through my stuff when I wasn't around. Thought I didn't know, seeing that everything was already in such disarray. But I knew, as we understand our own bedevilment. There's a kind of fuzzy logic behind everything.

In the suitcase I had an unsmoked spliff. Heavy stuff which I intended saving for a special occasion. I removed it and stuffed it in my back pocket. There wasn't anything special in my life anyway.

I removed the burglar bars. I had sawn them off a long time ago and they were basically just décor now.

I hopped through the window and

strolled on in the dark past the fruit trees. I could still hear Kelly hammering on my door. How she cried for me to open up.

In the corner of the yard there was a Wendy house, where we kept the gardening tools. I sat down behind the house, made myself comfortable on the ground and lit the spliff. Its mellow sweetness rushed through my body.

Peace at last.

I watched the tip glow. Then I lay down on my side on the ground. While gently floating away I wondered what Kerbs and Sky were up to. If they also thought about Partygirl.

The dreams came fast and furious.

One of them was more like a voice and probably not a real dream. At first the voice was far away. Then it came closer. It called . . . my name . . .

'Burns . . . ' The word echoed in my mind.

It was Partygirl.

'Burns, I am not dead.'

TRACK 23

Lost

I woke up, soaking with sweat. The Wendy house's wall was against my back and the ground right at my face. It was still dark.

'I'm not dead.'

I glanced around. It felt as if the voice had whispered it in my ears just now. Maybe shouted, because it was still so clear. It couldn't have been a dream.

She was there!

Partygirl was alive.

I have to find her, I thought. I jumped up, felt my stomach aching with hunger pangs. The munchies. But fuck that, I thought, I had to find her.

'Partygirl!' I cried out into the night, stumbling around in-between the trees. 'Partygirl!'

My voice echoed against the neighbours' houses, returning to me in the dark, abandoned and empty.

I climbed through my bedroom window. She might be waiting for me in my room. No, she wasn't there either. I threw open my cupboard door. Nothing.

My heart raced as if I had run the Comrades marathon in a record time. Anxiety thickened in my throat, stole my breath. I unlocked my bedroom door and darted through the house. From room to room. I called her name. Screamed her name.

Nothing.

'Chris!' someone called my name. I turned around.

It was Kelly.

'Have you lost it completely? What's going on with you? Just look at you!'

Only then did I notice how filthy my clothes were – from the sweat and the sand. My skin was sticky and there was sand under my fingernails. My mouth tasted bitter as if a dog had lifted its leg inside it. I felt sick, nauseous and hungry.

Lost.

Empty.

Kelly stared at me as if I were roadkill.

'Why didn't you open up the door earlier?'

'She isn't here,' I said.

'I wanted to talk to you. Shit, I just want to talk to someone. You know you can't with Mom – '

'She isn't here.'

'They're getting a divorce, Chris. And what will happen to – '

'She isn't –'

'Mom's with the other guy, Chris. I know she's not here.'

'Not Mom.'

'What? We've been talking about Mom the whole time!'

Kelly seemed to be hovering across the carpet. Past the TV, the hi-fi . . . hazy white like an angel.

'Chris!' Suddenly she was right back where she was before. In focus. It looked as if she wanted to cry.

'Go talk to one of your boyfriends, I don't wanna fucking know. I don't care what Mom and Dad do.'

'You're a real dick, do you know that?'

I know.

What would you do, Jack White?

Sunday felt like a dream. Kelly went to her boyfriend's. She had a whole bag full of stuff with her when she left. I didn't know if she would come back. My mom was probably still with her boyfriend, my dad probably at a friend's place or in a hotel.

He still hasn't come to fetch his car. Shit, I hoped he wasn't hanging somewhere in a hotel or lying in a tub with slit wrists.

No, he'd rather go drinking. Feeling sorry for himself. Trying to forget.

I trudged around in the house feeling anxious. She's alive, the thought rushed around in my mind. I was certain of it. I just had that gut feeling. I saw her hand moving in the tent. I thought then it was a trick of the light, but it wasn't. Her hand must've really moved.

I looked around for my cell phone. I had to phone Sky, to tell him. I found the phone on the carpet in the TV lounge. The TV was on. They showed re-runs of old animal programs. The presenter whispered excitedly as a cheetah chased down a springbuck, grabbing it by the throat, and pulling it to the ground. Dead.

Sky's phone rang and rang. The voicemail didn't even come on for me to leave a message.

I phoned again. The same story. Then I tried getting hold of Kerbs. After the second ring I hung up. No, I decided, leave Kerbs out of this. I shouldn't speak to him. Not now. I was still pissed off with him. (And that's putting it mildly.)

I stepped inside the kitchen to get

something to eat. Partygirl's face haunted my thoughts.

Show me your happies. And she really did. I smiled.

I knew she would show them to me again. Once we're alone. Like we were that Friday night. And this time Kerbs wouldn't come and fuck everything up. This time it would be perfect. She would lie in my arms and she would be mine. Mine, all mine.

While I was eating the sandwich I'd made, I typed a SMS.

i think partygirl is alive.

I sent it to Kerbs and Sky.

I sat waiting for fifteen minutes. Not one of them replied.

I went outside to remove the camping

gear from my dad's car. Whatever I could, I packed away. And whatever I couldn't, I hid away.

Entering the house, there still wasn't any reply to my SMS.

I went to my room and lay down on my bed whilst deciding what I should do.

'What would you have done, Jack White?' I asked the man with the pale face on the White Stripes poster. Jack White didn't reply.

I decided to go and look for Partygirl.

I saw her at least three times, somewhere, walking the streets of Bloem, but I couldn't stop in time to catch up with her. She also didn't come when I sounded the car's horn.

Kelly came back on Sunday morning. The bag of stuff that I thought she had packed to leave for good, hung over her shoulder. The boyfriend obviously had other plans.

My mom arrived shortly afterwards.

'You probably heard,' she said to me.

'Yes.'

'And?'

'And what, Mom? You can do as you please. What do I care?'

'You know your father and I . . .'

'I said I don't care. Leave me alone.'

She seemed too tired to fight. With me anyway. My dad arrived home later that night. Then all hell broke loose. Things were being smashed to pieces against the wall. Doors slammed. My dad pleaded for another chance. The whole soap-drama.

On and on and on.

Then he got in his car and drove off.

The cheetah had seized its prey and ripped out its throat.

Eventually everything comes to an end.

Lost anything?

Monday morning I woke up and decided to go back to Aldam. (Fuck school.) Partygirl came to me again the previous night. In my dreams.

Her hands moved across my body. I could feel her breasts against my back. Her legs folding around mine. Her fingers curling around my dick, starting to move slowly. 'I'm not dead, Burns,' she whispered. Like a freezing Free State winter night. When I woke up, my body was icy cold but dripping with sweat.

She was gone.

Only the cluttered room lay around me. And Jack and Meg White stared like ghosts from the red and black poster.

I had to go back to Aldam and take a look.

I had to find out what my dream meant. If it was true.

I tried phoning Sky again. He didn't answer. Where was he?

A guy in a pickup truck gave me a lift on the N1. He probably thought that I was going to sit at the back, but I thought – forget it, I'm not sitting in the wind all the way to Aldam. It was also looking like rain again.

I got in next to him. I saw his lips parting as if he wanted to say something. Perhaps wanting to protest. I pretended not to see it.

'I'm on my way to Aldam, and you?'

'Kroonstad.' His voice was uncertain. He probably didn't know what he'd let himself in for right now.

'All right then.'

He pulled away. I saw him glaring at me from the corner of his eye.

'You don't have any luggage,' he said.

'No.'

'What are you going to do at Allemanskraal Dam?' he asked with a heavy Afrikaans accent.

'Ah, you know.'

He frowned. I could see he wanted to know more, but bugger him, he wasn't my father.

When he saw I wasn't in the mood for chit chat, he switched on the radio. Radio Sonder Grense. Can you believe it? I thought all their listeners had bloody well died already. Well, that was how the presenters talked to them. As if they were scared to wake the dead, leaving that for the Second Coming.

'It's now ten o'clock and time for the news,' the presenter said in Afrikaans.

His words struck my mind like an echo in an empty room.

What if they carried a story about Partygirl on the news? About her disappearance from her mother's house. That she went missing. Perhaps something about a body that was found at the Allemanskraal Dam . . . Maybe that the police were on the lookout for three boys in their late teens that could help with the investigation. (Translated meaning: the guilty fuckers.)

The news reader drawled from one story to the next. Robert Mugabe who was still refusing to get off his throne like a full of shit teenager, giving the world the finger. The ANC protecting their wickets. The enormous Aids pandemic wiping out people all over Africa. (And the South African minister of health who wanted to stop it with garlic and beetroot.)

When a story about another farm attack came on the air, the old guy just said 'fuck' and switched off the radio.

Nothing about Partygirl.

We drove on in total silence. At the Aldam exit he dropped me off. I started walking to the gate. A game warden picked me up halfway and dropped me off at the resort's swimming pool. (I told him that my friends were waiting for me there. I couldn't really tell him that I came to see if we actually buried Partygirl.)

When he drove off I started making my way to the dam. Down the stone stairs, past the trampoline and put-put course, the new swimming pool and the super tube, to the camping area, where the main stage was.

Cleaners were already busy picking up

the rubbish. It looked like a dumping site: beer cans, papers, used condoms. The fine grass was in bad shape after the weekend. In places you could see the rectangles where the tents had been.

I tried working out where our tent stood. It was close to the water. I walked alongside the dam. Everything looked different. I stopped at a flat patch of ground. Was it here? It didn't look as if the ground had been tampered with. I looked at the area again. The trees in the distance. The distance from the main stage. (They were busy taking it down.) No, it wasn't there.

I strode further.

My heart missed a beat when I saw it.

Unmistakable for someone who knew, but if you didn't know, you would walk over it without noticing anything.

The ground made a slight bump even though we took a lot of it out and dumped it in other places. The Beetle's hubcap was still lying there. I picked it up, turned my back on the workers and wiped it clean with my T-shirt. Just in case there were some fingerprints on it. Then I dropped it again.

I stared at the ground. As if I wanted to say that I was sorry. I didn't mean it. Sorry, Partygirl.

But I didn't say it. I chased away all the thoughts that tried to surface in my mind, attempting to feel nothing.

It happened.

Live with it.

'Lost anything?' one of the cleaners suddenly asked behind me.

He would never know just how much.

TRACK 26

Something has changed

My mind was a mess as I lumbered back to the main building at the swimming pool. I saw nothing around me. Heard nothing. I only thought about her. About Partygirl.

I soon found myself sitting in a car and driving back to the gate along the resort's road. I must've stolen the car, I thought vaguely. But I couldn't remember doing it. In the rear-view mirror I noticed the small window at the back was broken. The loose wires from the hotwire job hung at my knees below the dashboard.

The car's entry ticket was sticking out of the ashtray. I handed it to the guard at the gate and quickly paid. 'Keep the change.'

I didn't want him getting too close to the car and having a better look. He might notice that there wasn't a key in the ignition. When he lifted the barrier, I drove out, relieved. I stepped on the gas pedal and the car roared forward.

The road back home was like a bad trip in which Partygirl didn't feature anymore.

A car turned off with me at the Nelson Mandela exit at Bloem. And right again to Langenhoven Park. It followed me through the streets. Past the Pick 'n Pay, down Dirk Opperman Street.

The car's windows were tinted but I recognized the car.

It was Kerbs.

Fuck knows, I didn't have the strength to deal with him.

My heart started racing, I didn't know why. We were friends. But something had changed. I felt it in my gut.

What did he want?

I stopped at the Caltex garage and left the car there.

Kerbs drove by. I saw him turning his head in my direction when he drove past me, his arm hanging out the open window.

I raised my hand to greet him but he had already turned his head away, his eyes fixed on the road.

I quickly started for home, on foot. I wished I could have just driven back to my house but I couldn't show up at home with a stolen car. It would have been plain stupid.

It was a long way home. I glanced back occasionally while still keeping my pace. Kerbs could have appeared behind me again at any moment. There were too many cars around. I tripped over a rock when the umpteenth car drove past and I glanced fearfully over my shoulder.

When I finally reached our road I quickened my pace. And then I saw it: Kerbs' car was parked on the sidewalk.

He was waiting for me.

Smaller steps. Smaller and smaller steps.

Something has changed.

Rapidly increasing heartbeat, sweat running down my back.

My eyes slipped out of focus, then back in focus.

What did he want?

I approached, saw the painted flames on the doors, the bumper sticker: *Just visiting this planet*. The word *Kerberos* was painted on the car's boot. Kerbs found it in a book. In the Greek mythology Kerberos was a hell hound with multiple heads that welcomed people to the realm of the dead. He had to see to it that they couldn't get back out again.

Kerbs got out of the car. He stood there in the open door, smiling in very much the same manner as Friday night, that devilish smirk.

'Where were you?' he asked. His voice sounded weird. Friendly and firm at the same time.

'Don't worry, I know,' he said before I could answer. 'You should stay away from there. You're gonna drop us all in the shit.'

'I had to go and look.'

'At what?'

'If she is really dead.'

'But you know that she's dead.'

'I saw her.'

'We all did.'

'Afterwards. When we came back.'

'You're talking shit and you know it.'

'No.'

Kerbs slammed the car door closed. He approached. 'And? Is she really dead?'

'The grave is still there.'

'But is she in the grave?' Again that unearthly laugh. Mocking, as if he knew the answer.

'I don't know. Probably. I couldn't dig it up, there were people.'

'Oh, you're fucked in the head, Burns. So let me help you.' He now stood right in front of me, forcing a whisper through his clenched teeth: 'She's fucking dead. We killed her and – '

'You killed her! We only helped to bury

her.'

'No, Burns, we did it. Remember? You took her first. Got your rocks off and everything. And then I took her, and then Sky —'

'Sky was outside the tent the entire time. He only saw her when she was dead already.'

'No, Burns. You've got it wrong. First you, then me, then Sky. And then you again. And you bashed her head against the gas cylinder. You were fucking wild, Burns. I couldn't believe it. Not from you, buddy.'

His words slashed through my mind. That wasn't how it happened. Fuck knows, it wasn't.

'No, Kerbs. It was you . . . it was you!' I yelled at him. 'Ask Sky. He'll tell you.'

'I'm afraid Sky can't say anything anymore.'

Ice cold words. Kerbs' eyes bore through mine. I suddenly realized what he was actually saying.

'Sky wanted to go to the pigs, Burns. He wanted to tell them what you've done. Squeal. I decided: to hell with it, you don't do that to your friends. I took care of him, Burns, for you . . .'

I had to swallow hard at the puke pushing up my throat. Shit, everything around me was falling apart. Kerbs slipped into focus, out of focus. His voice seemed far away.

'Don't worry, nobody will find him. And he won't be able to talk anymore. And neither should we. We should go on as if nothing happened. We don't know anything.' He grabbed my shirt and forcibly pulled me closer. 'We didn't see anything, didn't hear anything. Okay, Burnsie? Okay?'

I probably nodded, perhaps even said yes. I can't remember.

But Kerbs was satisfied. And that was all that mattered.

Brandy doesn't work

I went to bed with one of my dad's bottles of brandy. (Weird that he didn't take it with him, now that he was on that downhill slide.) Morning came and I decided to throw the empty bottle away when everyone had gone. Curled up in a ball it felt as if someone was playing a boyband CD backwards in my mind. (And no, it didn't sound any better.)

The sun shone through my window, directly onto my bed. I was still fighting against waking up. Why couldn't I just sleep? Forever and ever and ever. Then I wouldn't have to struggle through this wasted life. Everything was in turmoil. Broken, fucked up.

I thought about Sky who lay dead somewhere. What did Kerbs do to him? It would be something cruel. I knew Kerbs. He wouldn't settle for second-best, he would have made sure.

Sky always had a soft side. At times I wondered why he hung out with a guy like Kerbs. It was looking for trouble.

Come to think of it, I should've known that too. I did know it. That was why I befriended him. Because of the imminent possibility of danger. But I never thought that it would go that far.

I wondered if Sky knew that Kerbs was going to kill him. Did he see it coming? Probably not, otherwise he would have done something.

His parents were still in America. They probably hadn't been informed yet.

Should I go to the police? Should I tell them about Partygirl and Sky?

And Kerbs.

I shut my eyes.

Everything was fucked up.

There was coffee in the percolator when I stepped inside the kitchen. I poured myself a big mug. I thought about drinking it black, without sugar, but it tasted so bad that I tossed in the milk and sugar.

I thought I was seeing things when a strange man came through the door. Blond, sturdy, tall. Probably ten years older than me. He stared at me for a while without saying a word, got fruit juice from the fridge and poured himself a tall glass. I watched him the whole time. He sat down opposite me at the kitchen table.

'So, you're Chris?' he said.

'My dad taught me not to talk to strange guys.'

I had an idea who he was: Mom's

boyfriend. Fucking toy boy.

'Your dad isn't here anymore, is he?' said Toy Boy.

'And you think you are?'

He smiled, nodded his head.

'My name is – '

'I don't give a fuck what your name is.' I got up and made my way to the door. 'You screw around. That's all I need to know about you.'

'Anthony!' he called out after me. 'My name is Anthony!'

I slammed my bedroom door shut, put on a CD from KoRn – *Take a look in the mirror.*

I turned the volume way up.

I pulled a T-shirt over my head, dragged my fingers through my hair and grabbed my wallet. Kerbs said that nobody would find Sky but I wanted to go to his house and see for myself what was going on. Had he been murdered there? Then the place might still be covered in blood.

What would Kerbs have done with Sky's body?

'Where are you going?' my mom asked when I stepped out the front door.

'To town,' I said. 'I'm taking the bus.'

She continued talking but I wasn't listening. It couldn't be important anyway. And if it was, I just didn't care.

The security gate slid open. I quickly stepped through.

'I was wondering when you would come,' someone said behind me.

It was Sky.

TRACK 28

How do you tell someone that he is supposed to be dead?

My heart missed a beat. My whole body turned cold. I stood there unmoving, saying nothing. Feeling dead inside.

'You look as if you've seen a ghost,' said Sky. His voice sounded different. Normally he would laugh, but his face was solemn, expressionless. This frightened me even more.

He approached. I stepped back.

'But you . . .' The words vanished on my tongue. How do you tell someone that he is supposed to be dead? 'What are you doing here, Sky?'

Again he approached, again I stepped back, blinking my eyes. Perhaps he'd disappear. I tried thinking clearly. Tried figuring out what the hell was going on.

But Sky still remained in front of me. The living dead, or something like that.

'Has Kerbs been here yet?' asked Sky.

I nodded. 'What are you doing here?' I repeated.

'What did Kerbs say, Burns?'

I swallowed heavily. 'He said that you were dead . . .'

'Dead?' The old Sky would have smiled if I'd told him that. But not now. His expression stayed fixed like a TV newsreader's.

'Does it look like I'm dead?'

Fuck, yeah, I thought. Or perhaps not, I couldn't really tell. I didn't answer.

'I'm not dead, Burns.'

'Kerbs said he killed you because you wanted to run to the pigs. Wanted to tell them . . .'

'He told you a bunch of crap. You know him by now, don't you Burns?'

I still didn't know if I could believe him. He just looked so weird.

'Come take my hand, then you'll know.'

He held his hand out to me. I expected blood to come trickling down his sleeve any second, flesh falling away in his hand, leaving the bones exposed. Yellow white.

But that didn't happen.

I carefully reached out my hand. My heart started beating faster. Faster.

I touched him . . .

And my hand went right through his!

'Fuck!' I screamed and almost crashed to the floor.

'And now?' asked Sky. 'Why are you scared? This isn't anything new for you, is it?'

'Are you shitting me? Who are you?'

'Sky. You know that.'

'No.'

'Come on, Burns, we're buddies.'

'No.' I tried catching my breath. My eyes were glued to Sky. 'What do you want?'

'I came to warn you,' said Sky. 'One last time.'

'Warn? Against what? Do you still have those damn visions even though you're dead?'

'All the time, Burns. It's like a bad rash that won't go away.'

'Then what is it? Tell me so you can fuck off.'

'He's going to kill you.'

'Who? Kerbs?'

Sky nodded.

I stared at him. I didn't know if I should believe him.

'He's afraid that you're gonna tell. You already went back to Aldam. He didn't like that. The warning lights in his head already went off, Burns. He's got a plan for you. He knows how he's going to do it, where he's going to do it. Maybe he'll chop you up into little pieces. Maybe he'll feed you to the dogs, bit by bit."

'No, shut up, I don't want to know. Shit, why are you telling me all this? It's crap and you know it.'

'Have I ever been wrong, Burns?'

I kept quiet.

'You've got to get away, Burns. Far away. And you can't come back. Don't tell anyone where you're going. Kerbs will find out and he'll come for you and he will kill you. Even if you try hiding in the darkest alley in Hillbrow, he'll find you.'

I felt numb with despair. 'Where should I go?' My voice sounded weird to myself.

'Anywhere. But you have to hurry. He's on his way.'

What I know

I'm performing magic. Mind magic. And you're my volunteer.

That's what Sky had said in my dream. The one I had before we went to the MindFuck festival.

Was he still doing it? Was this what that was?

Or didn't I hear correctly? Did he say We're performing magic or I'm performing magic?

I couldn't remember. We would have made more sense. We – Kerbs and Sky.

They were up to something. I just didn't know what the fuck it was. My head was spinning. I tried reasoning but one thought just tripped over another. Like Grade 1 kiddies who all wanted to stand at the front of the queue.

Write it down. Write down what you know for certain, it's the only way you're going to think this thing through, I decided.

I tore a page from my Math book. (I should probably have gone back to school already. What day was it? It didn't really matter.)

The pencil case popped open in my hands as I tried opening it. I had to crawl behind my bed to find my pen.

With one hand I smoothed out the page.

Think.

Where did it all start? What happened first?

The white page cried out to me. Interrogated me.

Where?

Why?

Who?

What?

I tried thinking.

The first thing. What was the first thing? My mind didn't work anymore.

Write down only one word. One thing you know for certain, Burns.

One bloody word, Burns.

The page remained white. The pen sweated in my hand. I knew nothing, nothing, fucking nothing.

A sweat-, snot- or teardrop dripped onto the paper. The paper absorbed it, enlarging the stain.

Blood.

I wrote it down in outsized letters across the white paper. Scratched over the letters until they flowed into each other. Until the paper tore and I was eventually etching the word into the wooden desk.

That much I knew, there was blood.

That's what my dream said. That's what Sky said too.

There will be blood. And there was.

Or was there?

Doubt: the eighth sin.

Am I sure there was blood? I tried remembering how the blood flowed from Partygirl's head. I tried to remember what colour it was, what it smelled like, what it felt like. But the part of my brain that controlled the sight, smell and touch, had shut down. (It is now safe to turn off your computer.)

Then I didn't know it for sure. If there wasn't any blood, then it meant . . .

I crumpled the paper into a ball. Tore it apart, tossed it aside.

Blood was still etched on the desktop. I scratched it out with my pen. Just a bunch of lines. Out, out, damned spot. I smashed the pen to pieces against the wall.

I knew nothing.

Amazing to have arrived at this point and look back only to see nothing.

I grabbed a gym bag from my closet and started stuffing it full of clothes and other crap. Anything really. Sky was right. I had to get away. But not just away from Kerbs. From him as well. I had to start over. Clean slate. Somewhere where the people didn't know me. And I wouldn't get involved with people like Kerbs and Sky again.

A pain shot through my head. Instant headache.

More clothes, toothbrush, toothpaste. What else? I didn't know what else I needed because I didn't know where I was going.

Pain pulsed through my temples.

Blood that couldn't pass through the veins.

We're performing magic. Mind magic

And then, as if an angel had appeared out of the mist, I suddenly knew what Kerbs and Sky wanted to do. It was a game to them. Good cop, bad cop. Kerbs, the dangerous guy who was capable of murdering Partygirl and who tried desperately to pin it on me. Kerbs who lied and said that he had murdered Sky because he wanted to go to the cops. Sky who feigned warning me against Kerbs. Who wanted me out of the way. Perhaps they were both setting a trap for me so that they could kill me . . .

But why? I said that I would keep my mouth shut. They needn't have worried.

Then the answer flashed through my mind. The same reason Kerbs gave for killing Partygirl.

Because he could.

TRACK 30

dnuoranruT

The house suddenly felt like a cocoon, warm and suffocatingly dense with the silk threads closing in tighter around me.

I tried not to move my head too much. Perhaps it would help to get rid of the headache, I thought. I knocked back a few pain pills. Don't know how many. I just tipped the bottle in my mouth and swallowed. When they didn't all want to go down at once, I drank more water straight from the tap.

A pain was now burning in my stomach. But it was okay. At least now I knew what I had to do.

Why I had to do it.

I wondered if the car I'd stolen was still at the garage. Fuck, I hope nobody found it there.

'Chris.' It was Kelly. 'Are you going somewhere?'

'It's got nothing to do with you.'

'Chris, look at me.' I heard her gasping. 'What's wrong? You look like you came back from the dead.'

No shit, hey.

'Are you feeling okay?'

'Yeah, I'll be fine.'

Something inside me wanted to laugh at those words. I'll be fine. Damn, when? And will I? Will things turn around?

'Tell mom I left. I'm not coming back. She needn't worry. And tell dad that I'm sorry about mom and the other guy.'

'What?'

'Kelly, I can't talk to you right now. I'm in a hurry, okay?'

She grabbed me by my sleeve, pulling me back.

'You're going nowhere. Look at you. You're soaked, Chris.'

'Could be from the pills.'

'Which pills did you take?'

'Headache pills.'

'Bullshit, headache pills don't make you sweat.'

'Perhaps a few of them would.'

'How much did you take?'

'Dunno. Just leave me alone now, will

you? I have to get away. Kerbs and Sky are on their way. They . . . ' No, wait, I shouldn't tell her.

'Kerbs and Sky? Who are they?'

'You know.'

'No, I don't know. What the hell is going on with you?'

'They were my buddies.'

'Chris, you don't have buddies.'

'Yes, I do. Had. Kerbs and Sky . . .'

'Damn, it's happening again. We have to get Mom.' Kelly's face looked scared.

'Leave Mom out of this.'

'No, Chris, Mom has to come and help.'

'No!' I shouted. My head ached.

'Chris, calm down. It's happening

again.'

'What? What the fuck is happening again?'

'The things you see, Chris.' Her voice softened, eyes wide. 'You know . . . like last time.'

I kept staring at her, then she said: 'Kerbs and Sky don't exist, Chris. You don't have buddies. Remember? Everyone at school . . . they're afraid of you, Chris. Because you were in that hospital.'

'Hospital?'

'The fucking loony bin, Chris!'

The words struck me like a deadly blow, slamming me back against the wall.

TRACK 31

Proof

No, no, no. It couldn't be. Kerbs and Sky did exist. They were real people. Just like me. Just like Kelly.

I tried to understand what she said, but the puzzle pieces in my mind didn't fit together, as if they were jammed into the wrong spaces, jutting out angularly and skew. Making up a senseless picture of a life in turmoil.

'Chris?' said Kelly. Far off. 'Chris?'

'I don't believe you.' The saliva formed webs in my mouth. I swallowed it down. The pain still throbbed in my temples.

'I'll show you,' said Kelly.

I raised my head. She was scared too.

'Let's go look them up. We'll take my bike.'

I straightened up. Yes, I'd show her. Then she'd see. Kerbs and Sky were real people.

We had barely got on the scooter that Kelly called a bike, when I suddenly realised that I couldn't go with her. I leaped off the bike.

'Now what?' Kelly's voice was irritated.

'I can't go.'

'Damn, Chris, get on!'

'They're going to kill me, Kelly! I can't.' I screamed at her: 'That's why I need to fucking get away! They're going to kill me!'

'I want to help you, Chris. Trust me.'

'No.'

'Trust me.' Her eyes stared at me, pleadingly. 'You don't have to go in, you can stay outside. I'll go in and look.'

Trust me, trust me, trust me.

She sat on the bike, waiting for me.

I had to decide. She was right, I could hide away. They didn't have to see me.

I got back on the bike.

We drove to Sky's house first. It wasn't far from ours. I made Kelly stop at least a block away from the house. We didn't speak a word as we made our way up the road. She was a few steps ahead of me. I watched the heels of her shoes. They click-clicked on the road, rhythmically counting down the seconds. Like the beat of a song.

We reached the house, big and white. Now she would see. Then she'd believe me.

I stayed outside the yard, kneeling behind a tree. A car drove past. The driver stared at me. I turned my face away, the smell of the leaves filling my nostrils. I shifted forward to keep Kelly in my view. She marched up the driveway, ascended the stairs to the front door. Knocked and waited.

A woman opened the door. It was probably Sky's mother, but she seemed different. (Were they back from abroad?) She probably had a facelift.

I saw Kelly talking to her. The woman shook her head. No.

Kelly came back. Head lowered. I followed her down the street. She stopped when we were out of sight of the house, turned around.

'Chris, she said she's been living in that house for thirteen years. There's never been anyone like that there. She doesn't have any children.'

Every word was like a machete hacking off a piece of my body. Pieces of flesh dropping on the road behind me. Dogs sniffing at them, devouring them.

We drove to Kerbs' flat near Naval Hill. Kelly got into the old elevator. The metal gate rolled shut. Then the wooden door. Through the small window of the elevator I saw her leaving the ground floor, totally disappearing from view. I strode out to the inner court. After a while Kelly appeared in the corridor on the fourth floor. She hurried on over to the flat. Number 408. I only saw a part of her hair sticking out from behind the brick balcony, her head was turned away to the door.

She was probably knocking.

I waited.

She came walking back. That was quick. Too quick.

I waited for her at the lift. When the gate opened, she stood there with folded arms in the dim yellow light.

'The place is empty.'

No! I've been inside that flat myself. It wasn't empty. It couldn't be. She probably didn't bother taking a decent look. I rushed inside the lift. I needed to see for myself. Kelly had lied to me. Fuck, I hated her.

My fingers trembled. I looked for the right floor button but was unable to find it because I couldn't think straight. I pressed them all.

I saw Kelly crying.

The elevator stopped on every floor. My heartbeat increasing each time, the anxiety constricting my throat.

4th Floor.

I almost fell out the door, stumbled down the passage. Kerb's door came into view. It was olive green. I banged on the door. Continuously. Someone had to open.

'Look through the window,' said Kelly.

I looked. There were no curtains in front of the windows. The place was empty.

I knocked again. He had to be there.

'Kerbs!' I cried out. 'Fuck, Kerbs, open up!'

'Shut-up!' someone shouted from the floor below us. 'I'm working nightshift and I want to sleep!'

'Kerbs! Kerbs!'

'Shut-up! I'll call the landlord!'

'Come, Chris.' Kelly's voice was soft. She started walking back.

'No, I'll phone him. You can speak to him. Then you'll see. Maybe I'm just at the wrong place, my head is so messed up. Kelly, wait.'

I took out my cell phone. Searched for

Kerbs' number. I couldn't believe I shook so much.

The phone rang on the other side. Someone answered.

'Kerbs? Is that you?' I held the phone so that Kelly too could hear. She wanted proof. I would give her proof.

'Kerbs?'

'There isn't anybody here with that name,' the voice said on the other side. A man.

'You're talking shit, man. I've spoken to Kerbs before. On this number. I've sent him SMSs too.'

'Are you the guy who keeps sending me those SMSs?' His voice turned angry. 'If I find you I'll fuck you up. You just go on and on with the bloody things. I've let you know before that you've got the wrong number but you don't listen. You just won't stop.'

'But this is Kerbs' number.'

'There's no Kobus or Kerbs or whoever the hell around here. Do you hear me?' The line went dead.

Kelly placed her arm around me. She had difficulty getting me back into the elevator. Together we watched the light counting down the floors.

4-3-2-1.

Lift off.

In the end it's all lies, isn't it?

Kelly placed her arm around me when we made our way back to the motorbike. I brushed it from my shoulders.

'Just leave me the fuck alone!'

'We have to tell Mom.' Her voice was almost drowned out by the noise of a car that raced past. 'She would know what to do – '

'No. Leave Mom out of this. She'll take me back to that place. I don't want to go back, Kelly. I'm done with everything.'

'What do you mean?' She kept quiet for

a while. 'You're not going to do something stupid, are you?'

I knew her eyes searched mine for an answer. I deliberately turned my head away. I didn't know what I was going to do.

'Chris, promise me you – '

'I'm not promising one fucking thing, okay? Why should I make any promises?'

The anger in my body now mixed with anxiety. And self-hatred. And emptiness. Like a toxic drink hitting my bloodstream.

'You don't understand, do you, Kelly? They're my friends. Do you have any idea for how long? And now I find out that they were only in my head. How the fuck am I supposed to know what is real and what is not? How do I know you're standing in front of me? How?' I stepped closer to her. 'Perhaps I'd know if I touched you. But what if my mind only thinks that I am touching someone, but it's not real? What if my mind is lying to me about it too?'

I stood right in front of her, raising my hand. 'Perhaps I should slap you? Maybe it would prove to me you're real if I felt my hand burning. But my mind could be lying to me again and I might only be imagining my hand burning. Perhaps I would only imagine you turning your head away, crying. Do you see? I don't know anything. I can't believe anything.'

Kelly came closer again. I could tell that she didn't know what to say anymore. But she cried. And again she tried to put her arms around me.

'If you touch me again I'll beat you up, Kelly. I don't care if you're my sister or not. Leave me alone.'

She turned white with fear, stepped back immediately. I cried. And I didn't try to hold back the tears anymore.

'Go home, please. Leave me.'

For the very last time I looked up at the brown building that stood hidden behind the trees. And I wondered if it really was there. And how much of the things that I have seen never really existed.

'I have to tell Mom,' I heard Kelly call from behind as I walked away.

It probably didn't matter anymore.

I trudged on. The tar road was coarse beneath my sneakers. And the further I went, the more it felt as if a part of me was out of step. As if, slowly but surely, it marched on ahead of my body. And maybe it would break loose. Any moment now. All I had to do was wait. Because if it finally succeeded in breaking loose, it would all be over.

And then death would come.

Mercifully.

But it did not come.

In the end it was all just lies.

Then came the thought: if Kerbs and Sky were all in my mind . . . was there really a Partygirl?

Running on empty

Shit, shit, shit!

There was only one way of being certain: I had to go back to Aldam. And this time I couldn't just look at the flat piece of earth, I'd have to dig it open. Until I found her.

Or not.

I had to beg for some money to catch a bus back to the garage where the car was. It was the first time in my life that I'd had to ask strange people for money. And I hated it.

I made my way into the city centre.

That's were the most people were. I didn't look them in the eye when I asked.

And they were either stingy or bloody deaf – the whole lot of them. Mind you, if I'd have come across myself in the street, I wouldn't have given me money either. I looked like the facecloth a whore uses to wipe herself clean after each customer, I noticed in a shop window.

I tried a story about my-poor-mom-who-suddenly-fell-so-terribly-ill-at-home-and-i-had-to-get-to-her-very-quickly-to-take-her-to-the-doctor.

And eventually it worked. I got the bus money.

Bus stops are the gathering places of the city's abandoned, lost and other choice assorted people. Every one of them seemed to be on a vibe from the diesel fumes that clouded out from the black bus exhausts.

I found a seat at the back of the bus, avoiding the scrutinizing eyes alongside the pathway.

Our driver was Mad Max reincarnated; Bloem's streets were his Thunderdome.

The car I stole at Aldam was still parked at the garage. As if it was waiting for me to take it back.

I got in and started it again with the loose wires sparking between my fingers. I noticed the petrol gauge shivering at the bottom of the red. I hoped the car would make it back to the house. I needed to get some money to fill it up with petrol. I adjusted the rear-view mirror absent-mindedly. Searching for Kerbs' car.

Kerbs doesn't exist, said my inner voice.

And Partygirl? I asked him.

He didn't answer me.

I didn't know what I wanted. Did I want her to be alive? Or did I want her to be dead? Really dead, because that would have meant that she truly was there. A light at the end of the tunnel that would prove that I wasn't completely fucked up.

I didn't know.

The car thankfully reached the house.

Kelly wasn't back yet. She'd probably gone to my mom's workplace. I had to hurry before they found me there.

I went straight to my mom's room. I knew where she stashed away money for emergencies. And this was definitely one. How much did I need? About a hundred and fifty for petrol, sixty for the toll gate, thirty to enter the resort. And a little extra for in case. I took three hundred rand and placed the box in exactly the same spot where I had found it underneath my mom's clothes.

I grabbed a shovel from the garage. It would speed up the digging. And a flashlight if I had to dig in the dark.

After filling up the tank, I took the N1 North.

At Winburg it was as if the clouds reached closer to the road. Dark, blue grey. That was where we'd picked her up. I glanced back in the rear-view mirror as if I could still see her running up to the car. Her black hair waving behind her.

I could still imagine hearing her voice as I rolled down the window. But her words had already vanished. It was only the sense of her voice that remained.

I switched the car's lights on. It was getting very dark. Moments later the first drops exploded against the windscreen, at first only a few dotting the glass and distorting the view; then it poured down. The sharp smell of water on tar rushed in through the air vents. The car wipers cleared away the raindrops but it didn't help very much. The world before me was now white and misty.

I only noticed a bunch of traffic cops

packing up their gear and scrambling to their cars when I had almost passed them. If it hadn't been raining then, they would surely have pulled me over – the car's needle had been tripping around 140, 150 all the time.

A good sign?

The brown road sign indicating the Aldam exit was barely visible on the side of the road. The car's lights drifted to the right. I made my way along the curving road to the holiday resort.

It was a terrifying moment. I was nearly there but I wished the road could have been longer. For in the postponement of the moment there was a weird liberation. Maybe a way out.

The high thatch roof of the gate towered in front of me. The giant stop sign forced me to stop. I waited for the security guard to come. The windows of the cubicle were steamed over. So he had to be there. Perhaps he was sleeping. I rammed down on the horn and drove forward until I was underneath the thatched roof. The sleepy guard emerged from the cubicle. He had a clipboard in his hands and he frowned.

'Day visitor,' I said.

'Ntate?' he said questioningly. Which actually meant: What the fuck are you doing here? Can't you see it's raining?

Get moving, won't you? I wanted to order him; I didn't want to sit there all day. But I bit back the words; this was the place where I stole the very car I was sitting in. He might know about it by now.

He started writing down the car's number plate.

I should have changed the damn thing but I thought of it too late.

I studied his face, his eyes for a whim of recognition . . .

He kept on writing.

Nothing.

He approached the open window again and handed me his clipboard. 'Please write your name there, sir.' He indicated a blank section on the paper.

I jotted down a false name.

He tore loose my copy, handed it to me and walked away to raise the barrier.

I drove through and waved at him. Past the first obstacle.

In the rear-view mirror I saw him aiming for his cubicle, but then he stopped and turned around again. There was another car approaching.

I adjusted the rear-view mirror.

The rain lifted slightly, enough for me to see the black car coming up the road.

A shovel full of dirt

I'd recognise that car anywhere. In rain, hail or wind. Or even if flames came down from the heaven, I'd recognise it.

It was Kerbs.

So, he's back, my heart raced. I gulped. The anxiety shot from my spine to the tips of my fingers. My hands trembled on the steering wheel.

It couldn't be him, you are imagining things! something screamed inside of me.

But look! Fucking look! shouted another voice, even louder.

It felt as if every nerve in my body was being carved up with a deadly sharp Minora blade. Stay calm, just stay fucking calm. Go do what you came here for.

He'll go away, he doesn't exist. You know that by now, don't you?

I tried fixing my gaze on the road ahead of me, but my eyes unwillingly shot back to the rear-view mirror. Time and again. Searching.

And the questions flashed through my mind. The same questions over and over. Quick, just like rush-hour traffic on a highway in Jo'burg. Where was he? Did he take another road? Did he know what I came here for? How long has he been following me? All the way here my mind was caught up in other things. I was thinking about Partygirl.

He was out of sight now. It was all your imagination, said the voice.

I drove down the hill to the caravan

park. Over the speed bumps. The trees hung droopingly wet beside the road. Then the tar road ended and the gravel road started. It was still raining but not as hectically as before. I followed the gravel road for a while, and then stopped to try and find the spot where we had pitched our tent. Everything seemed different now.

I drove closer to the dam, then followed the curve of the water. It had to be around there. Perhaps I should get out, I thought. I stopped the car and got out in the rain, glancing back over my shoulder to see if the black car was approaching. It didn't look that way.

I strode forward. The ground was muddy beneath my feet. My eyes scanned over the dark brown earth. Puddles of water started forming, fresh green grass had emerged out of the mud.

And then . . . an area where the ground had given way. A subsidence in the form of a grave where the ground started caving in from the rain.

My eyes blinked uncontrollably while I paced up and down, up and down beside the sunken earth. My eyes were glued to the ground. It was here.

I swung around and darted back to the car. I got it going and quickly drove nearer, the thought of possibly getting stuck in the mud not even crossing my mind.

When I stopped, I leaned forward onto the steering wheel for a second. My body wanted to keep on going but I knew I had to calm down. It was the only way I could think clearly.

I felt sick now. And empty. The moment of truth.

Who are you, Burns?

Totally fucked up? Or would a girl's body be proof that I sometimes still had my senses together? That I too was alive.

And that she had lived.

I got out, opened the car's boot and took out the shovel.

The slamming of the boot still echoed in my mind when I turned the first sod. The mud sucked back on the shovel blade. I heaved the wet sandy soil aside and stuck the shovel back into the ground. Again and again. It was as if every shovel of dirt got heavier. I was becoming short of breath. But I kept on digging. I tried to quiet down the noise in my head. I needed calmness. As I imagined it would be like in the middle of the dam.

A deep silence.

When I straightened up after the umpteenth shovel to catch my breath I heard the rumbling of an engine. The black car came driving along the embankment, heading straight towards me.

Forever and ever love

It was as if he did it on purpose: driving slowly.

Because he knew what I thought, how I felt. And the longer he could postpone the meeting, the better it was for him. The more the anxiety would tighten my chest; fight-or-flight reactions play up against each other.

He stayed sitting in the car for a while. I saw him moving behind the tinted windows. I couldn't see his face, but I knew that he was watching me.

The door opened. Kerbs got out. Black

jeans, black T-shirt. He slammed the door shut, swaggered closer, really full of himself.

'Burns,' his voice grated. 'What are you doing, buddy?'

'Kerbs.'

'Surprised to see me?' he smiled. A treacherous smile. Like one would imagine a snake would smile if it could.

'What . . . what are you doing here?'

'Ah, you know, I was a bit bored, so I thought I'd come see what the fuck you are doing with yourself these days.' He looked at the pile of dirt, smiled again. 'If you kept your side of the bargain. Same old shit. You know.'

I swallowed, didn't answer him.

'And it seems like I came at just the right time. What the fuck are you doing, Burns?'

'What do you think?' I stuck the shovel in the ground, felt the mud sucking back the blade.

'Sky said you would come back to her again. Somehow he knows these things . . .'

'Leave Sky out of this.'

'Can't. He's just as much a part of what happened as you and me.' Then he shouted over his shoulder: 'Aren't you, Sky?'

The door on the car's passenger side opened up. Sky got out. Head lowered, but with his blue eyes staring out from the shadows of his eyebrows.

'Sky?' I asked.

'Burns. What's up?'

'It's like a family reunion, hey?' laughed Kerbs. 'Oh no, wait, wait. Someone is missing. Wait, let me see who it is . . . Partygirl!'

His words were blades slashing open the arteries in my arm.

'So, what do you think, Burns? Who's behind door number three?' He shot a glance over his shoulder to the car.

I looked at Sky. He avoided my eyes. I knew that he knew.

'Come on, Burns . . . Where's Partygirl? Is she lying underneath your feet? Or is she sitting in the car, waiting for you? Where do you want her to be?'

I stared at the car, then at the hole in the ground.

'I don't know.'

'Crap, Burns, you do know!' cried Sky. 'Listen to yourself. What is screaming out the loudest? Your head or your heart? Your heart wishes for her to be in the car, wishes for her to be alive, sort of alive . . . like Kerbs and I.' For a moment it seemed as if Sky's face expanded outwards. 'Your head wishes for her to be dead. Stretched out in the ground below your feet and genuinely dead. It would mean that you're not really as crazy as Kelly and all the other people say you are.'

Kerbs' smile broadened. 'Profoundly poetic what Sky said, isn't it, Burns? I couldn't have puked it better myself. So what do you say, Burnsie?'

'I don't know.'

I paced up and down alongside the pile of dirt. Again flooded with the rush hour traffic of muddled thoughts. I could feel my brain throbbing, feel it growing bigger and bigger, the pressure increasing inside my skull. And any minute now it would explode and I would collapse into this shallow grave. Then it would be over.

'What's it gonna be?' taunted Kerbs' voice.

'I don't fucking know, okay?' I shouted.

Now Kerbs and Sky were both laughing out loud.

'Allow me to help you then, Burnsie,' hissed Kerbs. And then he cried out in a booming voice that rolled over the wet earth and the water, resounding somewhere in the distance and came echoing back. 'Partygirl! Partygirl! Get up! Wake up, girl! Come on, come on!'

I shut my eyes tightly, felt my body tearing in two.

Then I opened my eyes, my terrified gaze fixed on the black car. Searching for movement inside the car, behind the tinted windows.

Minutes went by, by, by.

There was nothing.

The car's doors stayed closed, nothing happened.

'Mind magic, Burns,' said Sky. 'You

know what you want. You want to be sane. You want people to like you. And when that didn't happen, you created us.' Sky's voice was like the waves lapping on the edge of the dam. 'Look there, Burns.' With an outstretched finger he pointed at the hole I had been digging.

A piece of fabric showed. The sleeping bag, now wet and muddy.

I got down on my knees. Started to wipe away the dirt, bit by bit. And with every handful of dirt that I wiped away, more and more of the sleeping bag was revealed. It was clear that there was a human body inside. I zipped open the sleeping bag.

It was as if Partygirl was being born out of the earth.

'You did it, Burns. You alone,' rustled Sky's voice. 'It could have been so beautiful. Like in the movies. You could have loved her. And she could have loved you. She did say that, didn't she? But no one had ever told you that before her, right? And you thought that you didn't deserve it. Because she was like an angel. And angels don't love people like you. You thought she only said it because she didn't know you; after all you had only been together for one day. And if she found out who you really were, she would change her tune. And you needed to prevent that, right, Burns? You didn't want to show her who the real Chris Burns is. The guy with the darkness inside his head. The guy who creates people like he sees fit and then carries them around with him. Conjuring up stories about them so that it seems as if he at least has a life . . .

'All of this you realized when you rolled off her. After the two of you had sex and you looked at her. Your Angelgirl. And then you bashed her head in while she stared at you with her angel eyes that grew fainter and fainter with each blow. And her blood running down your fingers. And her love that would be yours forever and ever and ever, like in the movies.'

I'm still breathing

It was a voice from above that woke me up. But I kept still, lying there with my eyes closed.

'Is he dead?' asked the man's voice.

'I don't know. Have a look.'

I heard someone jumping into the hole.

'He's breathing.' The man tugged at my wet clothes. 'Hey, boy, are you okay?'

I opened my eyes. It was an old man. Probably a fisherman.

'Are you okay?' repeated his friend, who was still standing on the edge of the hole.

'Yes, I'm okay.'

'Why are you lying here in the hole?'

Partygirl! They would see her!

I moved my hands over the ground, felt the mud pushing in underneath my nails. The memory of Sky and Kerbs came rushing back like a tidal wave. But my head felt clear from all the crying.

She wasn't there. I jumped up.

'What are you looking for, did you lose something?'

It was the second time that I had stood there and someone had asked me that.

Then I saw it: the drag marks leading away from the edge of the hole into the water.

'No, nothing, sir. Nothing. I think I found what I was looking for."

'Where? In that hole? What's it for?'

'It's only a hole.'

'Only a hole?' The guy frowned. 'I'll never understand you young people. Let's go, Frank. I'm cold. The fish won't bite in this weather anyway; only thing you'll catch is a cold.'

His friend laughed at his stupid joke.

I watched as they walked away. Luckily they didn't see the drag marks.

Again I stared down at the place where she had been. Now I knew that she was real.

In a way it made me feel better, but then again . . . somewhere in my mind there was a sadness that slowly, like poison, spread through my body, paralysing my arms and legs.

I curled myself up in the hole again. From the deep water of the dam a distant voice called out to me, like in my dream: 'Burns . . . Chris . . .' The echoes washed over me, dissolving in the misty air.

The cold enveloping my body made me realise that I had to go home.

But first I had to take the stolen car back to the café. Perhaps the car's owners were still around. If not, someone would probably let them know that their car had been returned.

I hitched a ride back to Bloemfontein. It was a talkative man with an old car that picked me up. He spread a blanket over the seat and wanted to know what I was doing on this road. Why were my clothes covered in mud? And, and, and . . .

I didn't tell him everything.

He stopped at the Jakkelsdrif roadside

café to find out if they sell coffee. I waited outside for him and watched the cars speeding by on the N1.

It was the black car with the flames on the doors that caught my attention. The windows were rolled down. There were three people in the car.

One of them, the girl, waved at me.

The End

I waited in the hospital bed. My dad would be visiting me in a while. And later my mother, without her toy boy. He would remain in the car.

My dad eventually found a job. He now peddles TVs at Game. My mom started with divorce proceedings. And all was going well. They were geared for a Disney divorce. Clean, safe, quick. No surprises. All that was missing was the soundtrack by Phil Collins or Elton John. Something like:

The end came like a car crash
And if you ignored the broken bones
And flesh and blood

You'd have to say:
Now wasn't that fun?

The pills lay in my hand. I felt them getting soggy with sweat.

'You shouldn't drink it, Burns,' said Kerbs. 'Fuck, buddy, they're going to poison you with that shit.'

I stared at the trees outside my window. Kerbs sat with his back against the wall. Sky sat at the foot of the bed. And Angelgirl held my hand in her pale, pale hand.

'They found a girl in Aldam,' I said when the silence lasted too long. 'At first they reckoned she had drowned . . . but then they found this massive hole in her head.'

I sighed. And placed the sweaty pill on the tip of my tongue.

Swallowed.

CHAPTER 1

I am just 17 and my life is over. Head spinning, hands shaking, I need to throw up again. The lights are so bright I can only squint. I can hear people passing, but they're just blurs.

Sitting here, sweat carving lines through my make-up, I feel as if everyone is judging me. The seats either side of me are empty. People are standing, rather than sit next to me – the junkie. Funny, isn't it, that I'm drowning in a sea of people, but if I died in front of them, it'd be alone.

I came here with Mai-Ling but they took her away, through those clear plastic swing doors. She was totally out of it. I thought she had just partied too hard when she fell on the footpath and started throwing up. But then blood started trickling from her ears and nose and I panicked. I got her here as fast as I could but it was hard, no-one would help. I haven't seen her since and nobody's telling me what is happening.

You think I am self-pitying. You're thinking I'm another spoilt rich kid whose daddy gave her everything. Shit, they called the cops before they called my father!

The only time anyone comes near me is to question me again. They want to know everything but I can hardly think, let alone focus on what they are saying. I'm still too smashed to concentrate and they know it, but they keep hammering me. I don't care what they want to know, I just keep on back at them: "Is Mai-Ling OK? Is my friend alright?"

They act like they don't hear me.

On and on they go with the same fucking questions, "What did your friend take? What did she drink? When did she start losing consciousness?"

I keep saying to them, I've already told you everything – just leave me alone!

"Fuck, I'm going to throw up again!"

It's been half an hour since I spewed but my stomach won't settle. My father is still not here, even though I've called him like a million times. I have no-one and I'm scared.

"Carrie Jones?" a voice startles me from behind. As I turn I am face to face with two cops. I can hear the whole waiting room exhale. The cavalry has arrived! Someone to take the druggie away.

"Carrie?"

They want me to talk to them but the room is spinning and I can only hold my head in my hands and nod.

"I am Constable Adams and this is Constable Cummings, we need to ask you about what happened tonight."

Taking my hands from my face, the neon lights burn. I see a woman who could only be three or four years older than I am. The realisation is starting to hit me that I'm in a shit-load of trouble and things have gone way too far. If the police are here then something really terrible must have happened to Mai-Ling. Or am I still tripping and this is not real. But it feels real – too real.

I swallow hard to stop the tears, "Is Mai-Ling . . ?"

The Constable's face is blank as she glances at her partner. It is as if they are talking in some kind of silent code to each other.

"Is she alright?"

Still no answer.

"Is she?" I am screaming now, I need to know! "For Christ's sake, will someone tell me what is happening with Mai-Ling?"

My words have poured themselves into my tears and I can hardly catch my breath. "She was just pinging, right? You know, she's just high. She'll be okay now that she's spewed, right?"

The female cop sits down next to me and looks me straight in the eye. She's freaking me out. My heart is racing and sweat is pouring down my face. My hair is dripping wet and I can't stop shaking. She is still just staring at me like she's searching for a way to break the terrible news to me.

She puts her hand on my shoulder. "Mai-Ling is still unconscious. This is very serious. We don't know yet . . ."

Bone Song
SHERRYL CLARK
Melissa is running scared... and she daren't make friends or tell anyone her secret.

Breaking Dawn
DONNA SHELTON
Is friendship forever? Secrets, betrayal, remorse and suicide.

Don't Even Think It
HELEN ORME

One family's terrible secret.

Gun Dog
PETER LANCETT
Does having a gun make you someone? Does it make you strong or does it actually make you weak? Stevie is about to find out.

Marty's Diary
FRANCES CROSS
How to handle step-parents.

Seeing Red
PETER LANCETT
The pain and the pleasure of self-harm.

Stained
JOANNE HICHENS
Crystal is a teenage mum in despair. Can't anyone see the tragedy unfolding? Her only hope is Grace next door.

The Finer Points of Becoming Machine
EMILY ANDREWS
Emma is a mess, like her suicide attempt, but everyone wants her to get better, don't they?

The Only Brother
CAIAS WARD
Sibling rivalry doesn't end at the grave – Andrew is still angry with his only brother, so angry he's hitting out at everyone, including his dad.

The Questions Within
TERESA SCHAEFFER
Scared to be gay?

Ransom

Life at the **CUTTING EDGE**
For more gritty reads in the same series

See You on the Backlot
THOMAS NEALEIGH
Tony is 'Clown Prince of the Sideshow'. He has carnival in his blood, but the fun and laughter stops backstage.

Ecstasy
A C FLANAGAN
Carrie's supposedly dutiful friend, Mae-Ling, is fighting for her life after an ecstasy overdose. But Mae-Ling is not the only one hiding dark secrets.

Scarred Lions
FANIE VILJOEN
A scarred, man-eating lion prowls the game reserve. Will Buyisiwe survive? And heal the wounds from the past?

A Forgotten Tomorrow
TERESA SCHAEFFER
Savannah is alone, and haunted by painful memories. Can she learn to accept the things she cannot change?

Hanging in the Mist
PETER LANCETT
There's always a price to pay for being different.

Thrill Seekers
EDWINA SHAW
Douggie starts hearing voices, and there's nothing Brian can do as he watches his brother and his mates spiral out of control.

Rans:m